What The Fang

AN UNDEAD EVER AFTER NOVEL

STACEY KENNEDY

For Kayli.
You are my sunshine, my moon and all my stars.

Stacey Kennedy

www.staceykennedy.com

Edited by Lexi Smail

Copy Edited by Victoria Curran

Proofed by Paula Grundy

Cover Design by Regina Wamba

Manufactured in Canada

CHAPTER

One

MOST WITCHES FEARED VAMPIRES. I saw them as a business opportunity.

The bell above the old wooden door chimed as a tall, dark, and handsome vampire entered my pride and joy, Cauldron Boil Books. The bookshop, with the weathered crimson-colored door and wrought-iron sign, was on a block of prime real estate in Charleston, South Carolina. The old red-bricked building sat along a cobblestone road in the French Quarter. The only reason I could afford the place was because of the whispered rumors of the shop being haunted. Considering I'd never seen an angry ghost in the shop or in my apartment above, the ghost either liked me or had liked what I'd done to the place. But whatever the reason, I was glad. The last thing I needed in my life was a ghost.

The vampire greeted me with a brief nod as I placed the latest bestseller in the storefront window display. Outside, the night was hazy, the lights from the antique lampposts burning softly through the stifling humid air. I had no doubt many witches thought sleeping during the day and working at night seemed strange, but since Charleston didn't have a bookshop, I adjusted my schedule when I landed in the charming historic city, figuring everyone liked to read, even bloodsuckers.

Turned out I'd been right. Vampires loved books as much as they loved a smooth, willing neck. And the *willing* part hadn't always been the case.

The war between humans and vampires ended when humans realized they were greatly outmatched. Once a peace treaty was signed to end the two-month brutal war, the United States government handed over control of three cities to vampires: Charleston, New Orleans, and Savannah, the only three cities the vampires had requested since they felt most comfortable in historic cities. Likely, because many of them were as old as dirt. I hadn't met a vampire yet who liked modern living and skyscrapers. So, with the money my mother, Zara Farrington, left in her estate for me, I found the most Victorian building in Charleston and turned the little space into something that was all my own. Every detail— from the antique bookshelves in rows and around the perimeter of the square shop, to the thick vintage oak furniture in the small sitting area, to the Frankincense incense— were all to vampires' tastes, and my bank account had never looked better. My fridge no longer contained only hot dogs and leftover macaroni and cheese, but also had healthy food grown in my garden on the roof, and I hadn't eaten a hot dog in a year.

Leaving the vampire to browse the new releases on the table by the door, I approached the counter and turned on the radio.

"It's time for a new beginning. For vampires to no longer hide in small cities but to flourish in business, in government, in freedom. It's time for vampires to stand above, not below, humans."

The sound of Ezra von Stein's grating voice was equivalent to nails on a chalkboard. Vampires were as bad with politics as humans. Maybe even worse since vamps lived by a different code. There were no jails, no juries, no kindnesses.

You mess up. You die. That was the code of Ari von Stein, the current Vampire King of the United States, and Ezra's brother.

After the war ended, Ari created peace between vampires and humans by accepting the three cities gracefully, by declaring peace so no other lives were lost, and by enforcing a treaty that only willing humans were on the menu. Thus came the Vampire Human Rights Act, protecting humans' rights. For any blood given, they were paid a hefty sum by the vampires who employed them. Most vampires had grown used to drinking blood from a glass instead of sinking their fangs into a neck. Except Ari's brother, Ezra, had been gunning for Ari's position so he could destroy the laws Ari spent a decade building.

"What a load of horseshit," my best friend, Gwen, said, approaching from the back room with a box of new releases in her arms.

When I opened the shop three years ago, Gwen had applied for the job I'd posted online, and I'd hired her on the spot. While witches weren't supposed to befriend vampires, and typically stuck to their own coven, I'd never done things most witches did, and Gwen was the gravy to my biscuits. Her fangs glistened dangerously, but her heart was pure gold. She'd been turned into a vampire against her will when she was twenty-seven. Things like that didn't happen anymore, thankfully, not with the laws Ari had in place.

"Hush, you," I rebuked Gwen quietly. "No politics in the shop. It's bad for business." Everyone was on one side or the other, and no one seemed to see common sense anymore. The divide between vampires was a true, real, terrible thing.

The vampire kept his focus on the books ahead of him, and I breathed a sigh of relief when I changed the station and Taylor Swift belted out of the speakers. The last thing I needed was to start my night off with the endless politics that plague the United States. Turning to Gwen, I asked, "Better?"

"Much." Beginning to sing along, she took out some of the new hardcovers and headed off to sort them on the shelves.

I turned my attention back to the vampire standing at one of the bookcases. "Can I help you find anything in particular?" I asked him.

"I'm finding what I need, thank you." The vampire ran his fingers over the spines of the books. "You have a wonderful collection of suspense novels."

"Thank you. I try to keep up on the newest releases. Do you have a favorite author?"

He glanced over his shoulder and gave me a knowing grin. "Too many favorites to only name one."

I restrained my snort. When you're hundreds of years old, you've likely read a gazillion books. Vampires were immortal. Witches were not, but they did have much longer lifespans than humans. Most witches lived five hundred years or more. Powerful witches lived over a thousand years. The aging process slowed to a crawl once a witch turned twenty-one, after she passed the Summer Solstice Rite, a rite of passage for every witch. It took a few hundred years for a witch to look over fifty in human years. "Please let me know if you need any assistance."

He bowed. "I will, thank you, miss."

Determined to get ahead of my to-do list, I pulled some new stock out of the box on the floor and set to putting them out on the display. The new James Patterson would likely sell out quickly. Vampires loved a good mystery. I'd even sold two copies of *Twilight*. One to a vampire turned as a teenager, who had stars in her eyes over Edward. The other to an older gentleman who called it comedy. Nonetheless, my paranormal section wasn't nearly as stocked as the rest of the genres.

Once I returned behind the counter, the vampire headed my way. He'd chosen a few books, setting them down. The first book was Nora Roberts' latest. A vampire with a heart, always a sentiment that amazed me. "I haven't had a chance to read this one yet," I told him, scanning the barcode, catching a whiff of the strong aroma of his sandalwood cologne. "When you come again, please tell me what you thought of it."

He smiled, his fangs up close and personal now, his dark eyes guarded like he'd seen and done things that would break me. "I'll be glad to." He offered a thin plastic card. "I'm paying by credit."

I was leaning forward to reach for his credit card when he inhaled sharply. On his second, deeper inhale, he cut his gaze to my face. The vampire's eyes widened and darkened, death shining in their depths. I jerked my hand back, reeling under the hatred burning on his face, coldness sinking into my bones.

He didn't move, those animalistic eyes locked on my every move, every breath, and heat flushed my body red hot in warning.

Before I could get a word out, in a blink of an eye, he was out of the shop, the breeze of his departure causing my hair to flutter. The shop's door slammed shut, knocking over books in the window display. My hands shook as I clicked the cash register to cancel the order.

Gwen peeked around the bookcase. "What was that all about?"

"I have absolutely no idea." I breathed deeply, attempting to settle the racing of my heart.

Gwen smirked. "Well, it wouldn't be Charleston if something weird didn't happen every night."

"True," I agreed, but I couldn't push away the unease creeping over me. Never, in all my twenty-four years, had anyone ever looked at me like they hated my guts. Sure, when I first moved to Charleston, not all the vampires living in the town were warm and welcoming to a witch living among them, but they looked at me with disdain, not hatred. *Never* hatred.

Determined not to let the vampire ruin my night, I focused on getting set up for our special guest, Sophie Sands, a vampire author who'd recently made the *New York Times* Best Sellers list with her thriller.

I did a good job not thinking of the odd moment with the vampire, in the hours that passed. But the creepiness crawled back up my spine when Sophie began signing books for her fans. I scanned the crowd, seeing if that vampire from earlier had come back, but I saw only happy, adoring readers clamoring to meet Sophie, a gorgeous blonde vampire who belonged on a red carpet.

I handed Sophie another stack of books to sign when Gwen sidled up to me. She leaned against the bookcase, folding her arms across her T-shirt that read I MIGHT BE A VAMPIRE BUT THAT DOESN'T MEAN I HAVE TO BE A DICK ABOUT IT. "Finnick and I are hitting up the Blood Moon Festival tomorrow." The only night we were closed. "Want to come with?"

Finnick was the third in our friendship trio, and the only other vampire who truly welcomed me into Charleston. "Yes, of course! Unless—" The festival wasn't meant for witches. We didn't celebrate the blood moon, only the full moon. And the relationship between vampire and witch was a sticky one. Witches came from white magic, given from the Goddess. Vampires derived from dark magic. Prejudice over whose magic was stronger, purer, never went away, not even when there was peace with humans.

"Unless nothing," Gwen said, baring her fangs. "Don't let some stuffy vampires with dinosaur-aged views get in your head. You're as welcome there as anyone else."

My heart grew two sizes. "Okay, you're right. Carnival rides and candy apples sound like a perfect night off."

"Great," Gwen replied, pleased. "I'll let Finnick know. Do you need any more help here?"

I scanned the dozen customers left in the shop and glanced at the clock on the wall. Sunrise was an hour away. "Nah, go home. This should wrap up soon and I'll close shop."

"All right, bye, Boo." Gwen dropped a quick kiss on my cheek before heading for the door.

I smiled after her. The myth about sunlight and a stake through the heart killing vampires wasn't true. The only way a vampire died was from being burned by fire. Bullets, knives and any other weapon could injure a vampire, but with human blood, they'd recover in seconds. Except if the blade or bullet was silver, then healing took hours. Even a vampire on the brink of death would eventually heal if they had blood. But from what Gwen told me, the sun was just too bright, too hot, too uncomfortable.

"Another stack, please," Sophie said.

I blinked. Sophie held out her hand, frowning. "Sorry." I reached for another stack of hardcovers and handed them to her. At the annoyance in her sharp blue eyes, I stayed attentive on the job at hand, keeping my thoughts only on Sophie's needs until I thanked her for coming to the signing and shut the door behind her after the shop cleared out.

Everything hurt. My arms from holding and passing books. My legs from standing so long. Most of all, my feet.

I locked the front door and flipped the sign to closed, and then dragged my aching feet toward the counter, where I closed the cash register, taking the money to the safe in the office.

By the time I turned off all the lights and made my way toward the back stairs leading to my apartment, I was yawning. I stuck the key in the lock and the hair on my arms rose. Spinning around, I stared into the darkness at the front of the bookshop but heard nothing, *saw* nothing. Feeling like I was beginning to lose it, I turned to the lock again when I heard a laugh and smelled sandalwood. A hard wall of muscle hit my back before a hand covered my mouth, and an odd metallic smell filled my nose.

"Fighting is pointless," a low voice said.

My blood ran cold as I recognized that voice. The creep from earlier spun me around, forcing me to stare into dark eyes that stood out against his pale skin. "You're not going to scream. You're coming with me."

"Like hell I am," I growled, kneeing him in the groin. Vampire or not, he went down with a grunt. I ran for the front door, except another set of hands grabbed me, and another, and I discovered the bookshop's carpet tasted like gritty sand. Most witches would have called on their magic to defend them, but I, being magic-less, struggled and roared, until all I knew were hands on my body and pain. So much pain.

Help.

Help me.

Until, like a switch being turned off, the world went black.

When that switch turned back on, I had no recollection of how much time had passed but only knew that I was no longer outside my apartment or anywhere near my bookshop. I jolted up with a gasp, finding myself on a black leather couch in a Victorian sitting room with furniture I bet was older than the city of Charleston.

Someone cleared their throat.

I jerked my head toward the sound, finding the most gorgeous vampire I'd ever seen, sitting in a leather wingback chair. Obviously, when he'd been turned, he'd done manual labor. He clearly had a strong physique and black dress shirt, rolled up at the sleeves to reveal mouthwateringly muscular forearms, and I just bet he had an eight-pack beneath that fancy shirt. Even his black dress pants were tight against his thick thighs. His shiny jet-black hair was styled, and he didn't look older than thirty-five, but his shadowed gray eyes declared his age was far older.

"What is your name?" he asked. His voice was smooth and low, and damn near melted my bones.

"Shouldn't you know my name? You abducted me," I shot back.

His nostrils flared. "I won't ask again. What is your name?"

"Willa Farrington," I said, studying my abductor. The waves of power coming off him were near stifling. "And you are?"

A smirk. "Killian Constantine."

Oh fang. Killian wasn't an ordinary vampire, he was the Warden of Charleston, making him basically royalty in these parts. Each city had their own Vampire Sovereignty; Killian led Charleston's. He was the police, the judge, the jury, and he answered to only one person: Ari.

The sane part of my mind told me to stay quiet. The impulsive part controlled my lips. "You are the Warden of Charleston. How dare you attack me."

He cocked his head, his regard deepening. "I didn't attack you. The vampires who attacked you are dead."

I blinked.

Again.

And again.

"Wait. Are you telling me you rescued me?" I asked.

A nod.

I took a minute to really see my surroundings, suddenly coming to realize I was sitting in Killian Constantine's living room at the Manor, a sprawling plantation, where Killian and his guard lived and conducted business. I sank into the couch. Gwen had told me on more than one occasion, *"Piss off any vampire you want. I'll deal with them. Just not Killian Constantine. You don't want to get on his radar."*

I scoped out the exits when Killian asked, "What source is your magic?"

"I don't have any magic." I admitted my greatest flaw. "I

failed the Summer Solstice Rite." The rite showed a witch where her fate lay—some witches made potions, some held strong defensive magic and trained as protectors for the coven, and others simply worked for the coven, keeping the band of witches tight. The Goddess gave magic to witches, and witches gave back blessings to the Goddess through rituals. I sucked at all of it, and after I failed the rite, I was blacklisted and kicked out of my coven. Even though my Aunt Flora, the witch who raised me, was one of the strongest witches in the coven, she could do nothing to save me.

Killian's expression remained a mask of arrogant male annoyance. "Who is your coven?"

"I belonged to the Southeastern Coven." Witch covens were split into regions of the United States. The Southeastern headquarters was in Blowing Rock, North Carolina. And while witches never went to war with humans, when the vampires fought their war, witches came to the aid of humans to protect their cities with magic, finally outing themselves to a world that once burned witches at the stake. It had left bad blood between witches and vampires, but a peaceful relationship between humans and witches had been forged during that battle and remained strong. They'd received a televised apology for the murders of the Salem witches and compensation to the covens.

Killian arched an eyebrow. "You don't belong to your coven any longer?"

"Like I said, I failed the Summer Solstice Rite, so they banished me." I had no doubt that the second I moved into Charleston, I was on his radar, being the only witch in his city. "Shouldn't you know all this about me already?"

He held my stare for a long moment, his magic brushing across my skin like warm fingers I didn't hate caressing me.

All vampires had some ability gifted to them through dark magic. Gwen could shape-shift into a crow. Finnick could teleport himself by locking on to someone's location. But the older the vampire, the stronger the magic.

Killian's power made the air crackle.

"What I know is that you were a quiet witch who brought business to town," he eventually said. "I didn't object to your stay because of this." The air thickened as his power swept over me, no doubt searching for deceit or hidden magic. When the power dissipated, he leaned his elbows on his knees and leveled me with a hard look. "But you are not a quiet witch any longer."

"I am a quiet witch," I retorted, keeping the snippiness I felt out of my voice. "I did not abduct myself. Shouldn't you be out there finding out why those vampires attacked me?"

"I'm not certain I believe your story."

My anger flared. "What reason do I possibly have to lie? I've lived in Charleston without incident for three years."

A pause. A long, *long* pause. "You called to me telepathically for help."

Silence descended. Heavy silence filled with questions. I waited for him to laugh or do something to indicate he was joking. The silence continued.

"You've got to be wrong," I implored. "I have no magic. I couldn't have done that."

"You did."

I had no gifts, no power, no *anything*. "Impossible."

"Not impossible," he said dryly. "Since it happened."

I held his gaze, not finding any deception, only disbelief in what I was telling him. I felt the blood draining from my face. "What the fang is going on?"

CHAPTER
Two

SEATED IN HIS CHAIR, Killian stared at me for a good minute, the longest minute of my life, before he asked, "Are you questioning whether I'm telling you the truth?"

I walked a very dangerous line. Even the air seemed to grow heavy with the warning. "It's not that I don't believe you, but something else must be going on. I don't have magical abilities. I never have."

His gaze flashed with irritation, and with vampire speed, he stood in front of me. I gasped as he snatched my wrist in an unforgiving hold. The heat of his touch burned my skin, and as his magic brushed through my head, his memories soon flooded my thoughts.

"Help. Help me."

The soft voice laced with fear rattled in my head. I flew above the dark country road that passed in a blur. The wind roared as I soared through the air, the smell of flowers in my nostrils. The full moon lit up the night, but my vampire eyesight was as keen as my senses, and everything inside of me was alarmed.

"Help. Help me."

The words. That voice. It all wrapped around me, urging me to fly faster. The only voice that had ever slithered through my mind was that of my Sire …

"Help. Help me."

The words kept repeating again and again as an old farmhouse on the left drew my attention. I didn't question my instincts; the presence of the woman who belonged to that voice pulsed around me. I flew down the quarter-mile-long driveway, lined by magnolia trees, toward the plantation. I studied the house as I closed in; it appeared to be built in the early eighteen hundreds as were many of the houses in Charleston. I hit the ground and hadn't taken two steps before a vampire rushed out the door and flew off the steps, lunging at me.

I braced myself, readying for the hit. The new vampire had little chance to win this battle. Within a step, I latched on to the vampire's head, twisted, and proved my point by yanking my dagger out of the back of my pants and slicing his neck. As he fell, gurgling his regrets, I released a tendril of power to burn his body.

I charged up the steps, then rushed into the house. The air was static with energy, indicating three other vamps were here. And I smelled something else that laced my veins with hot rage.

The woman was a witch, not a human.

These vampires were committing the most unforgivable act in vampiric law. No vampires wanted a war with the witches. Death would come, fierce and brutal, and no city would survive. For that reason, witches and vampires held peace.

"You have no right to be here," a low voice snarled to my right.

The vampire was physically strong, but the weak air about him declared he'd not been turned all that long ago. "Where is the witch?" I demanded.

The vampire took a step forward. His fists clenched at his sides. "You have no authority here. Leave now."

"Charleston is under my protection, you fool." I rushed him at a speed this young vampire wouldn't be able to match. My hand wrapped around the vamp's neck, right before his eyes widened, then

... snap! *A slice with my dagger ended any further argument, and the smell of burnt flesh quickly filled the air.*

I proceeded through the lavishly decorated house. On my third step, I picked up shuffling below my feet. Following the energy to the basement door, I listened a moment, waited for the others to come. None came. Taking two steps at a time, I flew down the staircase, and froze, time slowing to a stop.

The witch lay on the floor, knocked out cold, covered in bruises. Vengeance burned in my blood.

"You think you have a right to her?"

I had sensed the two vampires approaching from behind before they spoke but waited for them to draw closer. "Who is responsible for this?" I asked.

"How is that any of your business?"

"What you've done here is wrong." I turned to the vamps and stepped in front of the witch to shelter her. None of the vampires I'd seen so far were from Charleston. "Since you're new vampires, I will let you claim stupidity. But you'll leave now and let me take her."

"We cannot allow that," the thinner of the two said.

I arched an eyebrow. "Indulge me as to the reason?"

Both vamps circled me and stared intently, confident I would soon be dead. "You're not privy to that information."

I didn't move from my position. These two fledglings didn't pose a threat. Their pacing displayed their lack of combat skills. Vampires didn't need to pace. They needed to hold, then strike with quick precision.

Too bad I wasn't in any mood to show them their mistakes. I didn't let them attack. I released a swift surge of power, flames circling up their legs until both vampires were dust on the cement ground.

I hesitated, listening for further threats but only heard mice scattering and the soft breathing of the witch. Lifting her in my arms, I smelled the drug used to incapacitate her. When I reached the outdoors, I leapt to the skies, the clouds whipping by, the wind drifting over my skin.

Within a few miles, I'd reached the Manor, a Greek Revival mansion that was headquarters for Charleston's Vampire Sovereignty, standing among mature trees draped with Spanish moss. I landed on the front porch and carried the witch through the main doors a second later. My guards rushed to my side. "It's fine," I told them. "Back to your posts." I entered the living room, placing her on the chaise and lifting my wrist to my mouth, biting down hard. I held her mouth open, blood seeping into her throat. Each time she swallowed, relief followed. Soon, the healing in my blood would eradicate the drug from her body, and the bruises would disappear.

Then she'd answer every damn question I had for her.

"Ew, I drank your blood," I said, the moment Killian's memory faded from my mind.

He gave me an incredulous look. "From that memory, *that* is what you're focusing on?"

"Of course, all of that was horrible," I said without hesitation. I'd never drunk blood in my life. *Filthy* was what I'd heard many times growing up about blood drinking. But I moved on. "Sorry, yes, thank you for coming to my rescue and"—I forced the next part out—"getting the drugs out of my system."

He nodded briefly. "Did you recognize any of the vampires who attacked you?"

"Just one of them," I answered. "He came into my bookshop earlier but rushed out like he'd seen a ghost. I don't know what happened, or why he came back." My gaze fell to the window where the sun was shining brightly. "Sorry, what time is it?"

"Ten o'clock."

I shot up out of the chaise like a rocket. "My dragon! I need to get home. Quick. He'll be so worried about me."

Killian rose, a wall of hard muscle before me. "You're not going anywhere until my questions have been answered."

Vampires were afraid of Killian, but I was not a vampire. He had no right to keep me here. I took a step toward him and straightened my shoulders. "I wouldn't care if you were the king of kings; no one comes between me and my dragon. If you want to ask more questions that I have no answers to, then you'll have to come with me."

"You will answer my questions now," he growled.

Maybe it was the lingering drugs in my system, or just the annoyance of being abducted, but a witch isn't a good witch if she's not resourceful. "Can I use your phone?"

"Why?"

"To check in on my dragon."

He sighed heavily, gesturing to a table on his right.

I used a landline to dial Finnick's phone number. When he answered, I said in a rush, "Don't ask questions. I need you to come get me."

Killian muttered a curse as Finnick appeared, teleporting himself into Killian's living room.

"You better have a good reason for interrupting me," Finnick snapped, wearing gray jogging pants slung low on his hips. His sandy-blond hair was messy, his shirt gone, revealing a toned physique, his blue eyes maddened. "I had an incredible date last night." Finnick loved sex. He had no preference for gender, appearances, or anything in between. He loved everyone and everybody as often as possible. "I was about a second away from getting my hands on Jeremy's massive—"

"You know Killian Constantine, I take it," I interrupted before he'd regret the next thing he said.

Finnick spun around. "Holy shit!" He slapped a hand over his mouth, glancing between Killian and me.

Guards rushed into the room on a wild breeze, their daggers aimed at Finnick's head.

"We're fine," Killian said, eerily calm, and just like *that*, the guards were gone.

Finnick visibly gulped, an unnecessary move for a vampire. He gave me a scowl before glancing at Killian, putting on the professional expression he relied on as a real estate agent. "Warden, please forgive me for not only what I was about to say but for also showing up at the Manor uninvited. I lock on to a person with my power and do not know the location ahead of time."

Killian's glare nearly burned us both where we stood. "Then get out."

"No, don't get out," I interjected, taking Finnick's stiff hand. "I need you to take me home. I was abducted this morning, drugged, and I need to get home to Ambrose."

Each word I said sharpened Finnick's gaze. "Are you hurt?" he asked, looking me over.

"I'm fine." I squeezed his hand tight. "But I really need to go home."

Finnick's eyes cut to Killian before returning hesitantly to me. "He doesn't look happy that I'm here. Did the Warden not want you to call for me?"

"No, he did not," Killian said through gritted teeth.

Finnick cringed. He released my hand to grip my shoulders. "Are you in immediate danger?"

"No," I answered, not liking where this was going.

"Is the Warden a threat to you?"

I took in the vampire, seething in annoyance, still sitting in his chair. "No, he's not an immediate threat." Although I wasn't so sure about what he'd do if I didn't give him the answers he wanted.

"I love you, Willa," Finnick said sweetly, dropping one of his warm kisses on my cheeks. "But I can't step on the Warden's toes, no matter how sexy those toes are." In true Finnick style, he set a hard stare on Killian. "Will you promise to get her home safely?"

"I will," Killian said.

"Okay, then," Finnick said. He gave me a smile full of pity before disappearing out of sight.

"Traitor," I grumbled, not ready to give in to anyone's demands. Luckily, my head didn't hurt because of ingesting Killian's healing blood, but all I wanted was to go to bed. I could figure this mess out after a good sleep. Ignoring the hard wall of muscle and power behind me, I headed for the front door I could see down the hallway.

When I opened the front door, drawing in the sweet, floral scent coming from the hundreds of magnolia trees in full bloom, I heard an insufferable sigh behind me.

"What are you doing now?" Killian asked.

"I'm walking home."

One step.

Another.

And another.

Then he cursed. "Come on, I'll fly you home."

I grinned. Maybe Killian was a nice guy after all.

Until I turned and saw him glaring at me.

"Then you will answer any further questions I have."

I didn't have a chance to glare back. His arm slid around my waist, drawing me in close. I caught his scent—pine trees in the thick of winter— a scent so pleasing, a sigh escaped me before he shot into the sky.

———

The road came up fast on the way down from the sky, but Killian landed in front of the bookshop as gently as he took off, the morning sun beating down on Charleston. Old vampires still didn't enjoy the sun, but they could stand it for short periods of time without issue.

I drew in a big, deep breath of his delicious aroma and stayed in his arms longer than necessary. Goddess, he smelled good, he felt good. I broke away, stepping back from the warmth of his power. His fingers dragged down my spine to my hip and lingered, drawing my attention to his face. His glowing eyes met mine, but the distrust in their depths extinguished any heat there.

I turned to the front door and realized I didn't have the keys. "I had locked the door when I closed up this morning." Through the door's window, I spotted the keys near the back door to my apartment on the floor. "The keys are in there."

"Step back," Killian said. He grabbed the handle and gave the door a hard push and the lock snapped, the wood shattering as the door opened.

"Why do I even bother with a lock?" I asked, stepping through the threshold.

"To keep the humans out," Killian said, following me inside.

Except Charleston didn't have any humans living in town. While there was a peace treaty between humans and vampires, humans were still wary, knowing they were food. Any humans involved with vampires long-term lived lavish but hidden lives. They came and went, enjoying the wealth earned from their blood donations away from the vampire-ruled cities. Every so often, humans would come for a weekend getaway to get a peek at the dangerous new world of Charleston, but those visits were rare.

Killian leaned the broken door against the doorway and then scanned the area. "Is this where you were attacked?"

"Yeah." I sighed at the broken bookshelf. "I need to—"

"I'll get someone here to repair the door and the bookshelf so you can reopen." He reached into his back pocket, taking out a cell phone and firing off a text.

Before I could take my next breath, two vampires appeared with cleaning supplies and a tool kit. Killian began giving them instructions, and I studied the gorgeous vampire, wondering if maybe he wasn't all grumpiness.

Until he opened his mouth again.

"I don't want your mess to become my mess."

"Believe me, it won't," I said, moving toward the door that led to my apartment. I grabbed the keys off the floor, and Killian followed me up the staircase to the next door. The second I opened it, light gray scales danced between my legs in a blur. "Okay, okay, I'm home. Stop, Ambrose, you're going to make yourself dizzy."

My dragon finally plopped his butt at my feet, smiling up at me, big sharp teeth glistening, his tongue dangling out the side of his mouth. Dragons hailed from the caves in the Carpathian Mountains in Romania but had been captured and tamed by magic wielders over the centuries. Before supernaturals came out to the world, dragons were hidden, only flown at night and kept safe in underground lairs. Now, for the safety of humans, dragons were bred selectively for temperament to make them more trainable, and very few supernaturals could pay the steep price a dragon cost. The laws were strict; dragons were not allowed to live in big cities, and every dragon was recorded with the Dragon Registry, a division of the Assembly. That was the governing body of witches. Each coven had a high priestess who led them, the strongest witch of the coven, and their rule among witches was final.

I knelt and kissed Ambrose's warm nose, finally feeling like the ground was returning beneath me. Most dragons only stayed Ambrose's size—on par with a border collie—for a couple of weeks, but Ambrose had flaws. We were alike in that regard. I never grew into my magic, and he never grew into his size or his flames.

"What's wrong with it?"

I whirled on Killian. "Pardon me?"

"The   dragon"—he   gestured   to   Ambrose—"what happened to it?"

"Nothing happened to him." I stroked Ambrose's head, and he got excited, sparks flying out of his mouth. I quickly tapped my knee, where smoke began to rise from the burnt fabric. "Ambrose is perfect just the way he is." I covered his ears. "He's just little, that's all."

Killian harrumphed.

Ignoring the hovering vampire, I scratched under Ambrose's chin—his favorite spot—before I rose and headed for the open galley kitchen behind the living room. My entire apartment could probably fit into Killian's living room, but I was proud of it nonetheless. I had warmed the small space by bringing the colors of nature inside.

"Would you like a drink? Wine? Beer? Blood?" Vampires still ate and drank and used the bathroom, but they wouldn't stay living without blood, and I always kept a couple of bags of blood for Gwen and Finnick.

"Beer is fine." Killian moved into the tiny living room that only fit a chair, a small couch and a television set next to the bay window. He took the big chair in the corner surrounded by indoor plants. No one had ever made the chair look small. Killian made it seem tiny.

I nuked Ambrose's gigantic steak in the microwave, removing all the bones since his little teeth couldn't manage to break them apart. The moment I set his bowl down, he pounced, and the meat was gone in the blink of an eye.

Trying to wrap my head around everything that had happened today, I moved to the window and opened it, letting Ambrose fly out to see about his business on the roof where I'd planted a patch of grass for him.

I took a beer from the fridge and poured a glass of wine for myself before returning to Killian. "All right, now you can ask me your questions," I said, giving him the beer, then taking a seat on the couch.

Killian blinked at Ambrose, who flew back through the window, jumped on the couch, and curled up on my lap. "How long have you had your dragon?" he finally asked before sipping his beer.

"I can't remember not having him." The dry wine tickled my cheeks as I drank. "From what I understand, my late mother"—who was once the high priestess of the South-eastern coven—"bought him as my protector when I was a child." Before he asked, I added, "And no, from what I hear, he wasn't always this size, he was smaller when she gifted him to me, but he stopped growing at this size."

Killian's eyebrow arched. "A protector?"

I stroked Ambrose's warm scales that were soft and fuzzy, not leathery like they should have been. "He might not be big, but he's mighty. He came to school with me every day and always kept me out of trouble. Why do you ask?"

Killian watched Ambrose intently. "I've never heard of a dragon not coming into his power."

His surprise wasn't unusual, and I shrugged. "Ambrose is a bit of a mystery, but he's my mystery and I love him to bits." Realizing how off topic we were, I got us back on track, wanting to polish off my glass of wine and head to bed after taking Ambrose back out to the roof so he could go for a fly around the city. "Are these the questions you really need answered?"

"No." Killian took another long draw from his beer and then set the bottle down on the coffee table. "Have you had any trouble with anyone lately?"

"Not a single one."

"Unhappy customers?"

"No."

"Disgruntled readers?"

"No."

"Obsessed fans of an author?"

I sighed. "No, I live a very quiet life. I don't make enemies. I'm a bookshop owner for fang sakes."

Killian leaned back in the chair. "Tonight, you were targeted. I need to find out why to ensure the safety of Charleston residents."

I got that, but … "If you ask me, this was nothing more than vampires attacking a witch they don't believe belongs in Charleston."

"A possibility." His hand carved through his thick hair, holding it back before releasing it.

"You don't think that's the case?" I asked.

His intense stare held mine. "I won't make assumptions. I want facts."

A headache loomed that had nothing to do with being drugged. I was exhausted. "Do your abilities allow you to view my memories too?"

A nod.

"Then why didn't you look into my mind to see what happened yourself?"

"Without permission, reading someone's thoughts or memories is a violation."

I opened my mouth to respond but closed it. Killian Constantine was full of surprises. I finally offered my hand. "I give my permission for you to view the incident."

His hand clasped mine, and power shot up my fingers, raising the hairs on my arms as the energy pulsated from his touch. "Think only of the memory," he said, his voice rough.

My eyes shut on their own accord, and I fought against the tingling feeling deep in my core at the warm, welcoming strength filling up the space around me. His hand tightening on mine, reminded me I'd welcomed him into my mind, and I snapped my thoughts to the memory from the moment I spotted the vampire putting down the Nora Roberts novel on the counter to when I woke up on Killian's chaise.

When the memory ended, I opened my eyes to see Killian's shimmering with power, the irises a bright silver. I got the feeling it wasn't because of my memory, but more his reaction to the same energy around us. Heady energy, the pulsating type a witch could lose herself in.

Not wanting to get in any deeper than I already was with

the Warden of Charleston, I pulled my hand away. "Like I told you, I didn't know any of the vampires who attacked me. They also didn't give a reason for the attack. All pointing to one conclusion—it was a random attack, based on prejudice."

The smoky gray slid back over Killian's eyes. "It does appear that way."

I let loose a breath. "Good." Edgy, and not particularly liking how I still felt jittery in his presence, I rose. "If that's all—"

"It's not."

I sighed heavily. "There's nothing more I can tell you, Killian. Nothing more I can show you."

He leaned back casually against the chair, stretching his arms out on the armrests like he belonged there. "You've mentioned your mother. Who is your father?"

"How is that any of your business?" I asked, returning to my seat.

"It's my business because you live in my city, Ms. Farrington."

I wanted to tell him to stuff his questions up his gorgeous, sexy ass, but he wasn't wrong. Killian ruled Charleston. Questions from him couldn't be avoided unless I wanted to get a lawyer—which I did not—or I left Charleston, my *home.* "Fair enough," I conceded. "To answer your question, I have no idea who my father is. He died when I was a witchling. My mother raised me inside the coven, but she was killed when I was four years old. My aunt, Flora, took over as high priestess after that and raised me, and when I was old enough to ask who my father was, she said she didn't know."

Killian never took his eyes off me. I fought against squirming. He was powerful and handsome, and I was not immune to his charm.

He finally broke to chug his beer, then he reached for his wallet. He tossed a business card on my coffee table.

"Instincts are rarely wrong. If your instincts tell you this wasn't personal, then I'm going to believe you."

"Thank you." Point for Willa.

He gestured at the card. "My number is on there. If anything comes up, if you feel scared or uneasy about anyone, call me."

"I will, thank you." I bent down to pick up Ambrose. His low rumble of happiness warmed the cold bits of my soul after the anxiety of the last few hours.

Killian headed for the door, and I followed him back down into the shop. His vampires were installing a new door.

He took a step outside onto the quiet street and into the sunny day when something occurred to me. "Wait!" I called.

Glancing over his shoulder, Killian asked, "Problem?"

"Is telepathy one of your gifts?"

"No."

The floor felt like it dropped out from under me. Again. "Then how did you hear me call for help?"

"A very good question," was all Killian said before he shot up to the sky, leaving my hair fluttering around my face.

CHAPTER
Three

"WAKEY-WAKEY, WITCHY-WITCHY."

I snorted, cracking open an eye, curled on my side in my double metal-framed platform bed. Finnick's face was right in front of mine, his lack of breathing on my face. "You know it's rude to come into someone's bedroom without an invite, right?" I croaked.

"Oh, please, you'd be so lucky to have me in your bedroom." He smacked my butt. Hard. "Get up. You've slept late. In case you've forgotten, it's the Blood Moon Festival." The only holiday in Charleston. Shops were closed. The entire city went to the festival. "And you have a shit ton of explaining to do."

I grabbed my mauve duvet and pulled it over my head. "Go without me."

I could hear his footsteps as he left my bedroom, and when he returned, another pair of feet had joined his.

The duvet was ripped away. Ambrose leapt up from where he'd been sleeping beside me and began sparking, his embers raining down on my cheeks. "Ow, it's okay, buddy."

"It's anything but okay, Willa," Gwen said, frowning down at me, looking as stunning as ever, wearing leather tights and a deep-red corset. "This is the biggest night of the year. You can't miss it." She crossed her arms, narrowing her eyes, which were surrounded by shades of gray eyeshadow and fake lashes. "Besides, Finnick told me you had an interesting evening with the Warden. Get up. Go shower. We'll have a drink ready for you when you get out."

I groaned, pushing myself up in bed, wearing my nightgown that read I'M A WITCH IN THE MORNING.

Finnick scowled at my nighty. "You need to get some sexier sleepwear. Pronto."

"My nightgown is just fine, thank you very much." I shoved him out of my room, and Gwen followed with Ambrose trotting after her. I heard them laughing in my living room—likely at my nightgown—and the opening of my fridge.

The same exhaustion headache that started when I woke up at Killian's house came back tenfold as I headed into my small bathroom. I could barely turn around. The toilet sat tight next to my sink with the oval mirror above it, and the claw-foot bathtub filled up most of the space. I slid back the shower curtain and turned on the water before lifting the lever to shift the water to the showerhead, the pipes clanging.

After Killian left the shop, I'd taken Ambrose for a fly, and sitting in my rooftop garden, I researched everything I could on telepathy. The ability was rare, certainly among witches. Many vampires had the ability, especially between a Sire and his fledgling. Which meant that ability didn't come from me. Killian was an old vampire; perhaps he was coming into a new power. By the time I shed my nightgown and stepped into the shower, I'd pushed the thoughts from my mind.

When I walked into the living room thirty minutes later, wearing jeans and a tight black tank top, my long, slightly wavy brown hair hanging loose, smoky makeup around my deep-blue eyes, both Gwen and Finnick were drinking their favorite lime margaritas, which were crimson from the added blood. Before I owned the shop and the apartment, a human had used the property for her chocolate store, and I would swear I could still smell the sweet sugariness filling the room. The window near the kitchen was open, and Ambrose was nowhere in sight, off for his night flight.

A steaming coffee waited for me on the coffee table. "Thanks."

"You're welcome," Gwen said from her spot on the couch. "Now sit and tell us everything."

So, I did, beginning when the creepy customer came into the shop and ran out, the part Gwen already knew, to when Killian left this morning, leaving me staring after him.

Gwen blinked twice when I finished. "I'm not actually sure where to begin," she said.

Finnick agreed with a nod. "I had no idea you'd been attacked when I saw you. You looked fine."

I swallowed a gulp of coffee, relishing the jolt of energy. "Killian gave me his blood to remove the drug from my system."

Gwen's mouth hung open.

Finnick fanned himself, fluttering his long eyelashes. "What I wouldn't give to have just a sip of Killian Constantine's blood."

I shuddered, trying desperately not to remind myself how, in his memory, I seemed to *want* his blood. "Believe me, I don't want a repeat."

"No fun," Finnick said with a salacious wink.

Gwen snorted at him and then said to me, "What happened to you is so scary. I feel terrible I left you at the shop alone."

"Don't," I retorted, lifting my mug to my lips. "They were bad vampires who obviously had a prejudice against me. You can't be there all the time." I took another sip of the coffee.

"You're right, I can't," Gwen said, averting her gaze to the margarita in her hands. "But it's wrong, regardless. I'm so sorry that happened to you."

"Thanks. But I'm okay. Nothing hurts. And I'm fine."

"Except that you're telepathically talking to the most powerful vampire in Charleston," Finnick pointed out.

"Well, yes, except *that*," I said.

"Any idea what that's about?" Gwen asked.

"Got me." I shrugged.

Ambrose flew back through the window and landed on my lap. His mouth was wide open, his sharp teeth gleaming in the light—aka his hungry face. *No luck finding a snack, then.* I set my glass down and scooped him up, kissing his head before heading into the kitchen to grab the chicken in the fridge. "I researched telepathy after Killian left. If witches have the gift, it's there from birth." I wished this was the first inkling of my magic appearing, but I refused to be disappointed in myself. I'd already spent years punishing myself for being different.

"This is so weird," Gwen finally offered. "Like, all of it."

"Right?" I nuked the chicken in the microwave, and while the hum filled the air, I glanced back and added, "The whole thing is unsettling." At the beeping of the microwave, Ambrose flew over. He buried his head in the bowl the moment I set it down. With Ambrose settled, I took a blueberry muffin I'd picked up at the bakery a couple of days ago from the box and returned to my spot on the couch. "But that's really all I know. Just a bunch of weird stuff happening with no answers."

Finnick asked, "Did the Warden seem concerned?"

"He seemed ... suspicious of me," I explained, ripping off a piece of the top of the muffin before devouring it. "Like I wasn't being truthful with him. Or that my story wasn't lining up. I let him into my memories, and once he saw what happened, he said I should contact him if anything or anyone unsettles me."

Finnick waggled his eyebrows. "Can you contact him for other reasons too?"

"Oh my Goddess, Finnick, do you think about anything else but sex?" I asked.

"Hell no," he snapped, tipping his margarita glass in my direction. "Come on, Willa, even you have to admit that vampire is gorgeous."

"I'm not saying that he isn't," I argued, a little ashamed how susceptible I was to the Warden's looks. Normally, a sexy face didn't interest me. "What I am saying is that there needs to be more than looks and he's got a wooden stake stuck up his butt."

Finnick fanned his face. "I'd like to stick something up his—"

"I'd like to hear you say that to the Warden's face," Gwen interjected.

Finnick rolled his eyes, turning to me. "You really wouldn't jump on *that* if you had the chance?"

"No, I wouldn't," I lied breezily because *damn!* I could still feel Killian's power rushing through me. I couldn't even imagine how that power would feel when passion was added into the equation. "Sure, Killian is nice on the eyes, but he's brooding and intense. I like my partners ... I don't know ... not thinking I'm a liar."

Gwen burst out laughing. "Your standards are so high."

I smiled at her.

Finnick added, "I'm not saying date him. I'm saying sleep with him. Trust me, the brooding and intense types make fantastic lovers."

"First of all, I only *talked* to Killian. Sex really wasn't on the table," I mused. "Second of all, I don't want complicated. Sex always makes things complicated." I'd taken a few human lovers from out of town, but they always got attached. *Always.* And I couldn't promise my heart to a human. We could never have offspring, and I hoped to have a whole house full of them. One day, secretly, I wished to find a warlock, and that would be my ticket back into a coven. But I wasn't even sure that was a dream worth having anymore. "So, like I said, Killian Constantine is not for me."

"Witches are weird," was Finnick's dry response.

"They are," Gwen agreed with him, "but in this case, I think Willa's right. The last thing you need is Killian all up in your life. He's powerful and influential, and a whole lot of trouble."

Finnick grinned devilishly. "The right kind of trouble."

"Oh my Goddess, stop!" I grabbed a pillow, tossing it at him. Finnick caught it and smiled back, and my insides warmed. I might not have magic. Or my coven. But I had Gwen, Finnick, and Ambrose, and that was enough for me. Done with all this nonsense, I said, "If we can stop talking about my sex life, wasn't there a festival to go to tonight?"

Gwen and Finnick turned to each other, downed their drinks, then smiled at me, their lips and teeth bloody. "Party time," they said in unison.

I secretly hoped that was the only blood I saw tonight.

———

Across town, the blood moon, with its reddish tinge, stood out in the starry night, eerily making it feel like trouble was brewing in Charleston. The festival was roaring with undead life when we arrived at the abandoned soccer fields to canned clown laughter, flashing light bulbs around multicolored signs, and loud music. On his leash next to me, Ambrose jumped up and down, fluttering his little wings in excitement. Screams echoed across the warm, dry night air.

While everyone seemed hopped up on magical blood, my stomach turned as I stared up the snack vendor: popcorn covered in blood, blood corn dogs, and funnel cake, drizzled with more blood. "Blood caramel apples." I groaned. "This wasn't exactly what I meant when I said I wanted a candy apple."

Gwen's sweet laugh wrapped around me as did her arms. She rested her chin on my shoulder and asked the attendant, "Could you possibly make her a candy apple without the blood?" She batted her eyelashes, pushing out her chest, amplifying the cleavage already poking out through the top of her corset.

If vamps could blush, this young vampire would be beet red. "Yeah, of course, no worries."

I smiled at her, and she winked. Gwen had vampires chasing after her constantly, but she was the exact opposite of Finnick, picky about who she took to her bed. Even more so about who she gave her heart to.

"A treat for later," Finnick said with a laugh, gesturing to the attendant.

Gwen nudged him with her elbow. "You might like the shy ones, but when a lover touches me, the last thing I want is his hand to shake with nerves."

"You and me both, girl," I said, giving Gwen a high five.

Finnick eyed the attendant. "Fine by me. I like turning the innocent ones wicked."

A couple of minutes later, I was a grinning fool eating my witch-appropriate candy apple, walking side by side with Gwen and Finnick, who shared a bloody popcorn, with Ambrose flying a little ahead. Some vampires gave him funny looks, but I suspected those were vampires from out of town. Everyone in Charleston knew Ambrose from the shop when I'd bring him to work when my night wasn't too busy. We were walking by the bumper cars, when Finnick rushed ahead in a blur to stick his head through a photo stand-in of Dracula.

He smiled. "How deadly handsome am I now?"

"You'd think you wouldn't be so starstruck over Dracula," I said, biting into the sugary sweetness. All vampires loved the story of the famous vampire. Sometimes I wondered if they loved it so much because Dracula was bloodthirsty and violent in a world where they were bound by strict social rules, but I kept that thought to myself.

"Oh, hush you," Finnick countered, taking his head out and frowning at the image. "Dracula is a God among vampires."

"A fictional God," I reminded him.

"Still a God," Finn purred.

I snickered, finishing my bite, then gestured to the corn maze. "Shall we?"

"We shall," Gwen said.

Finnick waved. "You lead the way."

I plodded off with Ambrose flying ahead of us, the leash fully extended, his little tail waving from side to side. Of course I led the way. With vampires' heightened sense of smell, they could find their way out of the maze without any effort at all. "So, the date the other night went well?" I asked Finnick.

He shoved his hands into his pockets and shrugged. "A perfect night, but the morning ended up the usual way."

"Let me guess, you got bored?" Gwen asked, tossing popcorn in her mouth as we went into the maze.

"Don't look at me like that." Finnick scowled, staying a little behind me as we came to a fork in the path. "I can't help it they get boring the next morning."

I turned right. "Do you think you'll ever get serious with anyone?" Finnick couldn't seem to stand anyone longer than a night.

"Not anytime soon," he muttered, grabbing a handful of popcorn from the bucket Gwen held. "I've got immortality ahead of me. Unless I find my *gemina flamma*, I can't see why I should bother putting in more effort."

Witches fell in love with warlocks the way humans fell in love with each other, naturally, though most witches were attracted to wealth and power. Vampires fell in love naturally, too, but they also had the ability to find a mirror soul or gemina flamma. The English translation: *twin flame*. No one really had it figured out, except that the souls were like mirrors, knowing each other fully. Some believed that it was a vampire's dark power that sparked this ability—that drew two vampires together to produce a powerful couple that could eventually produce children. Only old vampires had enough power to produce life from an undead body. *"Survival of the fittest,"* Gwen had told me once. Other vampires believed it was a soul-deep connection, where two souls belonged together, and no force could keep them apart. I never could shake the creepiness of it all. I liked the freedom of choosing my life partner, and I couldn't imagine accepting an arranged marriage, especially one created by dark magic.

"Makes sense," I said to Finnick. "It is sort of pointless to date and maybe fall in love with someone if you know fate might swoop in and change everything if you find your mirrored soul."

"I can't even imagine how heartbreaking that would be," Gwen muttered. "But it's not like there isn't a choice. If you do fall in love, there's always the bonding ceremony that connects magic and souls together. You'd never feel your gemina flamma even if you met them."

"That's what I'd do," I said.

Finnick rolled his eyes. "Yeah right, you, Ms. I-Date-No-One. Like you have any plans to fall in love."

"I do," I retorted, tugging on Ambrose's leash a little so he'd follow us to the left, down another long row of dry corn-stalks. I scrunched my nose against the smell of something rotting within the crops. "But it's a bit hard to find a suitable match when you live in a city full of vampires."

"I don't see the problem," Finnick said. "Vampires are far superior to warlocks," the only partner a witch ever bonded herself to so offspring would stay within the magical family.

Interspecies relationships were frowned upon on both sides. "Why don't you come over to the dark side?"

"You wish." I laughed, nudging my shoulder into him.

He suddenly stiffened, scanning the darkness ahead of us in the corn maze.

Gwen took a step forward, her fists clenched at her sides.

"What is it?" I asked, peering into the blackness, wishing I had some ability to let me know what was ahead of us.

Ambrose began spitting up embers, yanking against the leash. The hairs on the back of my neck rose with the warm breeze that blew by. Power sang on the air.

"Vampires," Gwen hissed, thrusting me behind her. "With silver."

I didn't have a chance to wonder if they were a threat because in a blink of an eye they stood before me. Five men, lips all pulled back, baring their fangs.

"Give her to us, and both of you can walk away," a dark-haired vampire sneered.

The ground felt like it was slipping out from under me with nothing to hold on to, as I realized something important far too late. I had been targeted, and they weren't ready to let me go. "What do you want with me?" I managed to choke out.

The vampire didn't acknowledge my question. To Gwen and Finnick, he asked, "What's your choice?"

"She's not going anywhere with you," Gwen snarled, giving me a hard push, sending me soaring backward. Ambrose's sparks were a trail of bright light as he went flying with me.

I hit the dirt with an *oof*, unable to make out a single body in front of me, only blurs of fists and kicks and grunts and blood, splatters of it being hurled in my direction. Both Gwen and Finnick were strong fighters; before the war began, every vampire was trained to kill with brutal efficiency.

I stared at the dirt waiting for a body to fall, praying it

wasn't a vampire I loved. The wind suddenly picked up, and a dark shadow crossed over the blood moon. Dust clouded my vision as that shadow landed in the middle of the fight, and a blast of power knocked me back. *Again.* Ambrose whimpered, and I lurched to grab him, holding him close.

It was over.

In the middle of the five vampires on the ground—one groaning, the other four not moving—Gwen and Finnick were covered in blood from head to toe, but the triumph in their eyes told me the blood didn't belong to them. Next to them, Killian stood like what Finnick had called him … *a God.* A vampire who gave his word to those who lived in his city and kept his vow.

He turned to me, blood dripping from his hands. "All right?"

"Yes," I managed to say before rushing to my feet and throwing myself at Gwen and Finnick, who wrapped their arms around me tight. "Oh my Goddess, are you both okay?"

"I'm confused, but fine," Finnick said.

"Me too," Gwen said.

I backed away from how they were looking at me, suddenly feeling like I'd grown a big, green, hairy wart on the end of my nose. I hugged Ambrose tighter, trying to hold on to a sense of reality. I was weightless, spinning out of control, as I felt Killian's power brush against my senses before the bodies at his feet burst into flames. Another vampire blinked into existence, wearing the Manor's uniform of black cargo pants and a black T-shirt.

"Take him home," Killian ordered.

The guard picked the remaining vampire attacker up by his shirt and immediately vanished.

A long stretch of silence followed, filled with unasked questions, until Killian's shoulders lowered like he'd calmed himself. Though when his gaze met mine, his eyes were glowing bright in the dark night. "From now on, until we understand why you're under attack, you're with me."

A stupid witch I was not. "I understand, but my bookshop—"

"I'll run the shop," Gwen said, sliding her hand around mine. "Go with Killian. Keep safe, Willa. Something really terrible is going on here."

I swallowed my fear, my blood chilled at the fright thick in my friend's voice.

Finnick, obviously reading my emotions, wrapped me tight in a hug and said in my ear, "We're here for you. A hundred percent. You need us, just call."

"Okay, yeah, okay," I said, unable to form words beyond that.

"Don't worry about anything," Gwen said, giving me a quick kiss on the cheek before releasing my hand. "The shop will be fine. Finnick and I will go to your place now and pack you a bag. Finnick can bring it to you at the Manor." Her brow wrinkled as she asked Killian, "If that is all right, Warden?"

A nod. "Of course."

"Thank you," I forced out. To Finnick. To Gwen. "Thank you for helping me."

Finnick gave me a gentle smile that usually reassured me but failed to do so now. "We love you, Willa. Please call us once you know what's going on."

"I will. Promise." I ignored the blood now streaking my cheek and stepped closer to Killian as he opened his arm for me. Not even his wintery pine aroma could warm the cold inside me.

With Ambrose in my arms, Killian wrapped me in his strong hold and had us airborne, flying away from the second weirdest night of my life.

CHAPTER
Four

THE MANOR, with its red brick and massive white Tuscan columns, was built during the first half of the twentieth century, Gwen had told me over wine one night.

The moment Killian landed on the porch, the dark wood double front doors opened, and a butler greeted Killian with a warm smile. "Welcome home, sir," the vampire, wearing a black suit and tie, said.

"Good evening, Brant." Killian gestured me inside. "Let's get you more comfortable."

With Ambrose still in my arms, I stepped over the threshold, and he followed me into the grand house. Killian led me up a sweeping curved staircase, past a guard armed to the teeth: silver daggers in every place he could have one. He wore black cargo pants and a black T-shirt, the same outfit as the rest of the guards, obviously the Manor uniform.

Killian kept walking until he reached the fourth door on the left and then opened it, soft light spilling out into the hallway. "You can shower in here," he said, walking through the immaculate bedroom, with beige walls and a dark oak ceiling. A large limestone fireplace blazed across from a king-size canopy bed with cream-colored silk drapery. He opened another door past the bed, revealing an en-suite bathroom. "I'll have your luggage brought up when it arrives."

"Thank you," I said, breathing past the hard rock in my stomach.

Killian studied me a moment, a frown pulling on the corners of his mouth before he set his gaze upon Ambrose. "I can take him down to get something to eat while you shower."

"I'm sure he'd"—Ambrose fluttered out of my arms, flying next to Killian, his tongue wagging—"love that. Thank you." I laughed.

Ambrose flew out the door a moment later, and Killian said, "Take your time."

When he shut the bedroom door behind him, I let myself feel the full weight of what had happened tonight. Nothing made any sense. Trying to understand what trouble I'd landed myself in, I went straight for the large bathroom with an elegant pedestal sink and a framed mirror above, stripping my clothes off and placing them all in the garbage. I did not even want to consider what else was covering me besides blood. I stepped into the all-glass shower, turned the water as hot as I could stand it and scrubbed every part of my body, a few times over, washing away the horrors of the night.

By the time I left the bathroom, the steam from my shower following me, there were a couple of suitcases on the floor near the bed. My trembling had eased, but my stomach was still rock hard as I unzipped a suitcase, mentally thanking Gwen and Finnick for packing just about every bit of clothing, shoes, and makeup I owned.

When I came out of the bedroom, dressed in jeans and a blouse, my wet hair now in a messy bun, I started at the two security guards next to my door. "Sorry," I gasped, placing my hand on my chest to keep my heart from exploding out of my chest. "I didn't expect you there."

Both vampires were all business. The one on the right said, "The Warden is waiting for you in the kitchen."

"Thank you." I took a step forward but then halted. "Sorry, where exactly is the kitchen?"

"Down the stairs, follow the hallway and it'll be on your left."

"Great. Thanks." I quickly made it downstairs, taking in the beautiful artwork I assumed was old and expensive hanging on the burgundy-painted walls, and I found to the left of the foyer was a library. The main hallway led to a double door entry for the dining room on the right, with a bathroom next to it. Farther down the hallway was the ballroom, where Gwen must have gone when she'd come to the Manor for grand parties held by Killian. Past that seemed to be an office.

"Drop it," I heard Killian snap.

I hurried my steps at Ambrose's deep, angry growl, and then stopped to take in the scene at the door into the chef's kitchen.

Next to the island, Ambrose had a massive steak in his mouth. Killian gripped the other end of it. "What's going on here?" I asked, hands on my hips.

Killian cursed, gripping the steak against Ambrose's tight hold. "The steak has bones, and I thought you might be less than happy if your dragon choked to death."

"Ambrose," I said in a firm voice, pointing at him. "Drop that steak right now. You'll die."

Ambrose spit it out and sat back on his butt with a huff.

"You're welcome for us saving your life," Killian snarled, glaring at Ambrose, who bared his teeth. To me, Killian said, much calmer, "He snatched it off the plate when I was cutting the other one up."

I waved my finger at Ambrose. "Naughty dragon." I sidled up next to Killian at the island. "He likes to push his boundaries. Sorry."

"You're not the one who should be sorry," Killian grumbled, frowning at Ambrose.

I fought back laughter at the two of them scowling at each other and took the slab of steak off the floor to the cutting board and began cutting out the bone. "I don't think he's realized that he's a little dragon and can't eat the bones." Once I'd tossed the bone into the garbage bin next to the island, I placed the bowl down and Ambrose dug in.

Killian stared down at Ambrose, looking at him like he was puzzle he couldn't quite figure out.

"Why do you keep looking at him like that?" I asked.

"He's odd."

I thrust my hands back on my hips. "Do you want to try that again?"

Killian's gaze cut to mine, the narrowing of his eyes slowly relaxing into amusement. "I'm not calling Ambrose odd," he corrected himself. "The fact that he's remained small and never matured is strange." He studied Ambrose again. "Did the coven ever have any theories on what happened to him?"

"None that I heard of."

"Interesting," was Killian's response before he finally turned away from Ambrose. "Come on. Let's go get you some answers."

"Can we just wait for Ambrose to—"

A breeze brushed my face, bringing a citrusy scent along with it as a vampire came into the kitchen. Handsome in a rugged way, he wore the same uniform as the other guards and had green eyes, stylish blond hair, and a gentle presence about him.

"Severin is the Captain of my Guard. He will not let anyone near Ambrose." Killian's mouth twitched. "Or let the dragon near any more steak."

Severin nodded. "He'll be safe with me, miss."

"Thanks," I said, feeling a tug on my heartstrings. I didn't like leaving Ambrose with anyone else, but if Killian had mind-linked with Severin just now, Killian was his Sire, so I trusted in that. "Can you take him outside after he's done eating, for a fly and to see about his business?"

"I do not mind," Severin said.

"Thank you," I said with a smile that I hoped showed my gratitude before following Killian through the kitchen and down a set of old stone stairs. They opened to what I assumed was the Manor's command center. Monitors lined the stone walls with computers beneath, where vampires worked. A few looked my way as I walked by, but no one dared to ask why a witch was in their workplace.

The hallway curved and then forked left and right. Killian stuck to the right, and the groaning became louder with every step I took.

Until I discovered who made those noises.

"You kept him alive?" I asked, cringing at the blood coating the vampire chained to the stone wall by his wrists. The fact that he wasn't trying to break free suggested magic also bound him. But it was the ire in his dark eyes that made me stumble. His hatred seemed to be directed right at me.

"You need answers," was Killian's dry reply.

Two guards stood next to the vampire, one female, one male: neither of whom I would enjoy messing with.

The female said, "He hasn't said a word."

"I suspected he wouldn't." Killian eyed the injured vampire, who would heal if given the time, and then turned to me. "He's yours to question, Willa."

I swallowed, refusing to show weakness. The vampire tracked my every step as I approached him. "Do you know me?" I asked, scrunching my nose against the sight of blood seeping from the wounds on his face.

His lips pressed tight for a whole second before he gave a bloodcurdling scream.

I nearly gagged at the smell of burnt flesh. A quick look

over my shoulder, and I could see Killian's eyes glowing with his magic, his power filling the room, burning the vampire from the inside out.

When the screaming stopped, Killian said calmly, as if he was ordering a blood latte, "Answer her."

The vampire dangled by the chains until his body began healing. "Yes, I know you."

"But I don't know you," I countered. "So, how exactly do you know me?"

Another pause.

He bowed against his bindings. His scream followed, his skin turning beet red.

"You're—" the vampire exclaimed, dangling from his chains. Until healing once again enabled him to lift his chin. "You're Ari von Stein's daughter."

I absorbed what I heard, meeting Killian's stare, finding his brow furrowed over stormy eyes.

"Impossible. She's a witch," Killian spat.

"Part witch," the vampire moaned, the chains rattling, "but also, part vampire."

Wind blasted around me, rustling my clothes and whipping my hair into my face. Killian had the vampire dangling a foot off the ground, a knife to his neck, blood leaking from the wound.

"No more games," Killian snarled in the vamp's face. "Tell me why you attacked her."

The vampire didn't dare move and wheezed, "We were hired to capture her and were told she is Ari von Stein's daughter and needed to be taken alive. That's it. That's all I know."

"Show me," Killian growled.

I remained rooted to the spot, the stone walls spinning around me, my stomach turning alongside them.

One second.

Then another.

And another.

Until Killian's blade was no longer at the vamp's throat, and he slumped to the ground. "Take him," Killian said to no one in particular.

In a whirl of wind, only Killian and I remained. He slowly turned, his expression revealing my worst fears.

Time stopped.

"No, it can't be true," I whispered, wrapping my arms around my middle. "I'm a witch." *I'm a witch. I'm a witch. I'm a witch.*

He took a step forward, reaching his hand out. "Willa."

"No," I snapped, taking a step back. "It can't be true. I'm a witch." The churning in my stomach only worsened as the room spun. I fought to remain on my feet. I ran, ran as fast as I could back to the bathroom I'd seen in the hallway. Ambrose was hot on my heels, obviously sensing my distress from wherever he had been, as I slammed the door behind me, hugged the toilet and vomited.

———

When my stomach eventually emptied, I made my way back to the bedroom, dropping onto the faux fur rug in front of the fireplace. I'd seen the truth in Killian's face, written into every sympathetic line—my father was a vampire. The birth of a mixed supernatural only happened between two strong, bonded supernaturals. And in that situation, their offspring was sometimes—*rarely*—born without magic, only inheriting a longer lifespan. Before the war, dating a supernatural not of your kind was frowned upon because it tainted the blood-lines. After the peace treaty, vampires were more open to the idea, since bringing white magic into their bloodlines typically made for stronger offspring, but witches remained against the idea of mixing white magic with a vampire's dark-ness. Any witch who did so was banished from their coven.

I slid my fingers through the soft fur of the rug, suddenly every question I ever had was being answered. The Goddess had punished my mother for bonding with a vampire and rejected gifting me with magic. I wasn't flawed, I was a mix of light and dark magic, not a purebred. A witch and a vampire without any gifts at all.

There was a soft knock on the door. I desperately tried to hide my emotions and failed miserably.

Another knock.

Then the door opened.

Killian regarded me sitting in a heap on the floor, his eyebrows lowered. He came into the room, shutting the door behind him. The wood in the hearth suddenly blazed with crackling fire from his power, and I'd never been so grateful for warmth.

"I'm sorry," I said, sliding a hand over Ambrose as he came to sit near me, staring up at me with sad eyes. "I'm not usually such a mess."

"Don't apologize," Killian said gently. He took a blanket off the bed and wrapped it around my shoulders before sitting in the chair next to the fireplace. "This is … a lot to take in."

"I don't even know what I feel right now." *Other than lost.* As if sensing that, Ambrose curled into my lap, his rumbly purr a comfort. "Do you believe what he's telling you without a doubt in your mind?"

A nod. "His memories cannot lie. The vampire that came to your bookshop smelled that you're from Ari's bloodline." He ran a hand across his jaw. "From what I saw in both memories, and since I cannot tell that you're from Ari's bloodline, I suspect magic is at play here. Whoever is looking for you has been spelled to catch Ari's scent."

"Spelled by who?"

"I did not see that in the memories."

"How could I not know I'm part vampire?"

"Your mother never told you that your father was a vampire?"

I swallowed the emotion in my throat. "I was young when my mother passed away. I don't even remember her, except for a few flashes of her face. I asked my aunt once about my father, but she said he was a warlock who had come to town and gone just as fast, leaving my mother heartbroken."

This didn't sit right. My aunt loved me. Regardless of the conditions of the Assembly that made her banish me, she had still cared for me deeply, gave me a wonderful home with many loving memories. "Maybe my mother never told her the truth, out of fear she wouldn't accept me. But my mother left me to my aunt when she passed away. She's my mother's only sister. Don't you think she would have told her the truth?"

Killian considered and eventually shook his head. "Not if your mother was worried about your aunt's reaction to your father being a vampire."

The fire crackled. Ambrose began snoring, and my stomach roiled again as I stroked his fluffy head. "I just can't believe any of this is true." Or what it meant for me if it were.

A comfortable silence settled in as I continued to run my hand along Ambrose's head and down his back. Poor baby. Too much excitement for one night. Even I felt the drag of exhaustion, but there would be no sleeping, not until I knew what was real and what wasn't.

"I was given immortal life against my will."

At the pain in Killian's voice, I glanced up. His head was bowed, the orange hues of the fire cast a glow over his face.

"But had I not been given immorality, I would have died on the battlefield during the American Civil War." That meant Killian was over 160 years old. My twenty-four years seemed inconsequential. "My lieutenant discovered me after the battle ended, a broken Union soldier on the brink of death.

He had a choice: let me die or turn me to save me, but the choice wasn't mine."

I couldn't even imagine. "Did you wake up on the battlefield?"

"No," he answered, shaking his head. "I woke up in a farmhouse to a new life I had not been aware existed."

"Wait," I said and paused, "you didn't know about vampires before then?"

"I did not."

"Wow," I breathed. "You must have been so angry once you discovered what your Sire had done to you."

"What I felt was beyond any anger I'd known as a human. Not that I had been turned, but that my Sire had stolen my right to die a brave death in war. He'd stolen my pride in fighting to make my country better—to see the world without slavery, without hate, without prejudice."

"I get that," I said gently. "But you did see the world that way. The Union won the war; slavery was abolished."

The fire crackled, drawing Killian's gaze. "That's true, we did win, and had my Sire not turned me, I never would have seen it. I would have died that night, an unknown soldier."

My hand froze on Ambrose's back. "What happened after you were rebirthed?"

Killian's intense stare met mine again. "When my anger eventually turned into acceptance, I realized there was more I could do for my brothers-in-arms, more to be done in the world. And that is why I accepted the role of Warden in Charleston. To never forget why my brothers were slaughtered on that battlefield. To never forget the vision they had for a new world, a *better* world." He hesitated. "From the day I met my Sire, he's given me nothing but a strong, unwavering friendship. Back when I was turned, he gave me a choice to stay with him or go out on my own. He offered me freedom."

"What did you choose?"

"I stayed by his side because he deserved that loyalty, instead of going home to tell my family and my young fiancée of my vampirism and beg them to accept me. My Sire fought for the good of the world, for kindness when sometimes it became impossible to see what was right or wrong. He fought to make this world better, and he does so every night, not only for vampires, but for humans and witches, without once asking for anything in return."

My heart lodged in my throat. "Who is your Sire?"

"Ari von Stein."

Even the fire seemed to go quiet. "My father turned you?"

Killian inclined his head. "I hadn't known Ari was a vampire when he was my lieutenant. I only knew he was a leader and wanted a better world. His views aligned with my own." Killian paused, years of history gleaming in his expression. "I tell you my story because I want you to know firsthand the vampire your father is. Not only to me, but to every vampire in his bloodline or who willingly offers their life to protect him. He's fair, he's generous, his integrity is above reproach, and I have no doubt he'd want to meet the daughter he does not know about."

Ambrose shifted under my hand, purring again as I stroked him. "How are you so certain Ari doesn't know about me?"

"He would have told me," Killian replied without hesitation.

The wind rattled the window behind me, and Ambrose opened one of his eyes before he purred and shut it again. "You're that close to Ari?"

"Yes."

I regarded Killian and I believed him. But one thing didn't add up. "You're making this seem like it's my choice to meet Ari or not."

Killian leaned forward, resting his elbows on his knees. "It is your choice. I will not force you."

I tilted my head and paused, watching him closely for any hint of deceit. I found none. "You'd choose my wishes over your Sire's?"

He pushed up the sleeves of his dress shirt, revealing the tight skin stretching across the bulging muscles on his forearms. "In this case, yes, and Ari would want me to."

I allowed myself a good look at the flexing strength he offered before I stared into his smoky eyes locked on me. Killian was a cold-blooded, ruthless killer, but he was also proving himself ... honorable. "I'll never outrun this if I truly am Ari's daughter," I said more to myself than him. "There is nowhere to hide, and for some reason, someone is after me because of my connection to Ari." I heard the shakiness of my voice but pushed on. "I need to get answers, and they are likely with Ari."

Killian rose. "I suspect that's the best way forward as well. Until we know why someone has targeted you, being with Ari is the safest place for you to stay. I'll arrange a meeting with him." Killian went to turn away but then stopped, looking back at me. "You're not alone in this, Willa. We'll see this through to the very end. Until you can return to your bookshop and your quiet life, I will not stop until these threats are removed. That is my promise to you."

Emotion clawed up my throat. "Thank you," I breathed, my body releasing all its stored-up tension. "Thank you for helping me."

A tender smile filled his face with unexpected warmth, softening all his hard edges. Everything I knew and had learned about Killian suddenly blew apart, because it became clear that no one truly knew Killian, not the way I was beginning to know him. And as he shut the door behind him, I couldn't remember the reason I thought Killian was off limits.

CHAPTER

Five

I GAVE myself ten minutes to feel every bit of the weight of the truth that not only was my father alive, but that he was the Vampire King, before I picked myself up off the floor. Thoughts rattled through my mind at rapid speed; so many things were not adding up. How did Ari not know I existed? But the loudest thought of all was why Flora would hide the truth of my father from me, especially after my mother passed away? My aunt had shared her heart with me, it didn't make sense she wouldn't share this.

Determined to find answers, I left the bedroom, seeing the same guard waiting at the end of the hallway. "Hi," I said as Ambrose fluttered next to me. "Do you know where I can find Killian?"

"He's in his office, miss," the guard, with the piercing blue eyes, answered. "Down the stairs, follow the hallway, and it'll be at the very end."

"Great, thanks." I smiled, but then hesitated. "Should I request a meeting?" Killian was the Warden after all.

The vampire's eyes crinkled in amusement. "The Warden already knows you're coming and has indicated I send you down."

Right. Every vampire in this mansion would have heard our conversation no matter where they were. "Well, again, thanks."

"Anytime," he said with a proper nod.

"Come on, Ambrose," I called. He flew ahead of me as I moved slowly down the staircase. The Manor had mid-century modern furniture filling up the large rooms. A gold-and-deep-red carpet led my way down the hallway, the hardwood floor creaking beneath my feet as I padded past all the rooms I'd seen earlier. A warm light spilled out into the hallway, coming from opened double doors, drawing me forward.

I found Killian sitting behind a classic cherrywood desk, looking at paperwork. Behind him was a large painting of the battlefield of the American Civil War. On either side of that, dark wood bookshelves were lined with old books and obvious keepsakes from Killian's long life.

"Feeling better?" he asked as I met his gaze.

"Much, thank you," I said.

He gestured to the client chair. "Please take a seat."

Right as my butt hit the cushion, a slight breeze fluttered my hair, and then a teacup was being offered to me from one of the serving staff. I leaned forward, sniffing at the air. "Peppermint?"

"To settle your stomach," Killian said.

I smiled, accepting the tea from the server and thanked her before I asked Killian, "Isn't knowing about teas a little too witchy for you?"

He leaned back against his big leather chair, his mouth twitching. "I might have done some research on the subject after leaving you in the room."

Warmth settled across me as sweet as the tea and I took a long, slow sip, inhaling at the same time. But my tea wasn't the only sweet thing in this room, this vampire was warming other parts of me too. "Thank you for the tea," I said, after returning the teacup to the saucer on the small table next to me.

The slight incline of his head was his only show of accepting gratitude.

Ambrose flew onto Killian's desk, sniffed at him, and then curled on top of the papers, promptly sighing in bliss.

"He's also part cat," I said to Killian, which earned me a low chuckle. "Did you manage to arrange the meeting with Ari?"

"I don't need to call Ari," Killian explained, finally looking up from the dragon on his desk. "He is my Sire. Distance does not hinder our ability to mind-link."

Truth be told, I didn't know much about vampires beyond what I was taught during my schooling and what I learned from Gwen and Finnick after moving to Charleston. "Because you're both old, strong vampires?" I asked.

A nod. "Younger vampires in a bloodline still have a telepathic connection with their Sire, but they'd need to be physically close to converse."

"I see." I reached for my tea again, taking another lingering, heavenly sip. "So, you did talk to him, then?"

"I did. Right now, your father is in Savannah, sorting out a problem there, but he'll return to the Citadel tonight. We will go there to see him."

"And then what?" I dared to ask.

Killian watched me closely and then shook his head, causing strands of his hair to brush his eyebrow. "I'm afraid I don't have that answer for you. We're going to have to take this step by step until we understand why you've been attacked."

"I agree," I said. "But you think meeting Ari is the first step to getting these answers?"

"At the moment, I'm only thinking of your safety. The Citadel has security we won't find elsewhere. Until you get answers, you will be safe there."

Something now twisted in my gut. "Will you leave me there?"

Another pause. Longer this time. Nothing showed on his expression, his emotions locked up tight. "You belong to Charleston, Willa; therefore, it is my right to stay with you if that is what you choose."

I wasn't sure if my emotions were just raw, or if I was overly needy with all that had happened, but my next words came easily. "If you could stay, I would appreciate that. I … I just—"

"You don't need to explain yourself," he said. "You've been through a lot, and you'll go through more. I'll be there, with you, until you tell me to go."

I breathed a big sigh of relief. I couldn't really understand why I trusted Killian so naturally, I didn't even know him. I wondered if Gwen and Finnick's high regard of their Warden helped, or maybe all the stories I'd heard of Killian's honor to Charleston, and from what I had seen with my own eyes, but I did trust Killian. It occurred to me that I did need someone with me who I knew for certain had nothing to gain from me and would tell me the truth, because I did not trust Ari. "Can we do one thing before we go to Ari's?"

"Anything," Killian stated.

I glanced at Ambrose, who was watching me intently with his sharp eyes, like he knew where my heart lay. "Can we go to my coven to see Aunt Flora?"

"Why?" Killian asked with an arched brow.

I crossed my legs. "I need to know if she knew the truth about my heritage."

I heard voices from the hallway, but Killian paid them no attention, scraping a hand against his jaw. "Will she be honest with you?"

"I'd have no reason to not think so," I replied. "Flora raised me. She's been loving and kind and affectionate. But at the same time, she had to know that Ari was my father. I've seen the photographs of my mother and her growing up, until a couple years before she died. They were incredibly close."

Killian cocked his head. "But there's more to you wanting to go there."

I hated to even put this out there, but … "I know you trust Ari, and are fond of him, but I don't know him. I know my aunt, and I can't help but think that perhaps there is a reason she never told me about Ari being my father."

"You think she was protecting you?" Killian offered.

"I don't know, but I definitely think I should find out before going to Ari's house." I paused, shifting in my seat. "I know that puts you in an awkward situation because of your loyalty to Ari. I can go to Flora's alone."

"The truth is the truth, and we will find it." Killian rose, coming around to meet me at the chair. "We'll take some guards with us. Like I said, one step at a time."

I stood, stepping into the power emanating from him, finding only resounding strength in his features. My head stopped working, and I suddenly threw my arms around his neck, holding him tight. Then my brain caught up with my arms, and I froze. That wintery aroma … my body temperature turned up a few degrees.

I expected Killian to move away, to do something completely opposite of what he did do. He locked his arms around me, wrapping me in hard muscle and sizzling magic. "What is this for?" he asked, his voice rumbling in my ear.

"You didn't need to be this nice to me," I said, unable to step out of his arms and not wanting to, anyway. After the last days of confusion and fear, the solid wall that was Killian Constantine felt … *good.* "For the help, the protection, the kindness, and even the thoughtful tea, thank you."

His hug deepened, encasing me entirely. "You are most welcome, Willa."

My insides turned to mush at the way he tasted my name,

tasted it on his tongue. But then there was movement around my legs, and Ambrose was pushing his way between Killian and I, until he was in my arms and kissing my face. I laughed. "He gets jealous. He likes hugs a lot."

Killian watched as Ambrose's tongue flicked across my skin and then his gorgeous, simmering eyes met mine. "I can see why."

"Sir."

The spell around us broke, and I gasped, spinning to find Severin standing in the doorway.

"We are ready."

Killian's tender gaze met mine. "Are you ready?"

I kissed Ambrose's wet nose, then set him down, and he flew around Killian's feet. "I better be."

It turned out Killian had a powerful teleporter within his guard. Without even touching us, he teleported Killian, Ambrose and me, along with four of the guards for extra protection, five miles away from Blowing Rock. Since I wasn't sure what the coven would do if they sensed a group of vampires teleporting into town, and worried they'd attack first and ask questions later, we opted to teleport out of town and enter through the security checkpoint, which was the only road that led to the coven's headquarters. Also home to my Aunt Flora. Killian had SUVs waiting when we arrived, on the dark country road. We took one of the Escalades, while his guards drove in another.

After we hit the road, hugged by thick forests, Killian asked, "Is Blowing Rock where you grew up?"

"I lived with Flora in her house at the coven until I turned six," I replied, settling back into the leather seat, stretching out my legs. "After that, I went to the Assembly for my schooling, but I'd come home to Flora's for holidays and things like that. I haven't been home for a long time."

After a pause, he raised one eyebrow. "Charleston is your home, is it not?"

I smiled at that truth. "Yes, you're right, Charleston is my home."

His tender smile made me catch my breath, and I studied him, *really* studied him. Everything Killian had said and done for me since I'd met him ... all the stories Gwen and Finnick told me about Killian over the years were of his strict, no-nonsense, fierce attitude. That he was so committed to Ari and his duties guarding Charleston that he'd never bonded. There had been no rumors of his lovers. But the vampire sitting next to me wasn't a cold, aloof, disconnected, cruel vampire.

A low chuckle drew me out of my thoughts. "Is there something on my face I should be aware of?"

I blinked, suddenly realizing I'd been gawking at him. "No, sorry, there's nothing on your face."

"Don't be sorry," he said, his hand slung over the steering wheel. "What is it?"

I nearly kept the thought to myself but found I didn't want to. I wanted to know what made this vampire click. "If we're being honest here, you're just so different than what I was expecting."

Shadows crossed his face from the streetlights we drove beneath. "How so?"

"Everyone in Charleston is afraid of you."

He didn't even flinch. "Good."

"But ... you're not scary at all." Killian glanced sidelong at me, and I quickly added, "Okay, fine, you are certainly intimidating, but you're not the strict, cold-blooded killer that everyone thinks you are. And I'm sorry I was staring at you."

His voice lowered an octave as he said, "I don't recall saying that I minded you looking at me."

Unexpected heat touched unexpected places as I leaned over the console toward him. "Oh? The big, bad Warden isn't afraid of a little witch in his life?"

His gaze met mine. The bright silver color of his power glowed, simmering. "Do I look afraid of you?"

No, he did not. He looked like a vampire who knew his worth, and I couldn't help but wonder how that confidence would look as he stroked my body. Burning need flushed through me.

His nostrils flared, jaw muscles flexed, but he focused back on the road.

I breathed deeply, quickly reminding myself that vampires smelled desire like a human could smell bread baking. The ability came from the need to, at one time, lure a human to feed. It made for an easy target. I stared out the front window, fighting this foreign desire Killian brought out in me. Sure, I had met many warlocks and humans who I thought were attractive. Some I even took home for the night to enjoy. The warlock who had taken my virginity, Mikkel Wildes, I had dated from seventeen to twenty-one, but when I failed the rite, I apparently failed him too. But no one had ever stirred this simmering hunger in my core that felt like a living, breathing entity, a curious thing.

Ambrose gave a slow, rumbly purr in my lap. I ran my hand over his head and down his furry back, smiling down at him. Teleporting was always hard on Ambrose.

"To answer you," Killian said, breaking the silence, "there is a reason I keep a cold distance from those living in town. I need order and obedience to keep Charleston safe. For that, I will protect and lead them, I don't want the vampires living there to know me personally."

His eyes met mine again briefly, causing my breath to catch in my throat.

But I want you to know me.

The statement hung in the air between us. I parted my lips

to say *something,* when out of nowhere, lights suddenly blinded me, and time came to a grinding halt. A vehicle smashed into the SUV on Killian's side, sending us screeching sideways across the road, until another hit rammed us from behind. Glass shattered, but I realized none hit me because Killian's jacket had been thrown over top of me and Ambrose.

Before the SUV even stopped, I was ripped out of the car window, my seat belt burning across my shoulder as it gave way. A scream tore from my throat as I lost hold of Ambrose, whose roar had me fighting against the hands pinning me. I couldn't break free of the iron grip, so I turned my head and bit down on the vamp's arm as hard as I could muster. The vampire shouted a curse, letting go for a second, and I landed on the road with a hard *thud.*

Ambrose was fighting a vampire who kept trying to grab hold of him, his teeth shredding the vampire's arms. Beyond them, all I saw was a blur of bodies—so many bodies—all fighting Killian's guard and the Warden himself, his flowing power making the air thick. The smell of burning rubber clogging my nose, I pushed myself up off the road, when a vampire grabbed my foot. I flipped around and kicked him in the face. He cursed again as blood dripped from his nose. This time, when he came at me again, I kicked him in the groin and jumped to my feet, not even sure where to go, what to do.

"Willa," Killian roared. "Run."

I couldn't make him out or tell if he and his guard were winning or losing the fight. My heart told me to stay, to fight, but I could do nothing to help him. I spun away to run when I was tackled from behind. The pebbles on the road cut into my palms as I tried to drag myself forward, but there was no getting out of this vampire's hold. No saving myself. "Killian," I screamed.

A wave of power blasted out, dropping bloody bodies to the ground around me. Killian stood in the middle of the gore, his radiant silver eyes glowing in the darkness, and I knew there was no walking away from this. The anger raging on his face said as much, right before a dozen vampires jumped him. He and his guard were only five vampires, with more than fifty vampires here to attack them. An entire army had come to stop us before we entered the safe haven of the coven.

My heartbeat felt sluggish as I screamed into the battle, screamed for the lives that would end tonight, screamed at the unfairness. In a speed my eyes couldn't register, the vampire caging me to the road lifted me in his arms and was dragging me toward an awaiting car.

"Killian," I screamed, knowing it was pointless. He could not help me. No one could.

But as I shrieked against that truth, the vampire holding me suddenly bowed in pain, dropping me when a blur of silver pounced. The smell of burning flesh infused the air as Ambrose's sparks burned the vampire's cheeks and he tore the vampire's face apart.

"Ambrose, no," I bellowed, lurching to save him.

The vampire backhanded Ambrose down the road. He did not get up.

I cried out as my heart shattered, screaming for help.

A blast of power knocked me backward into the ditch.

"Not the witch or the dragon," Killian yelled, but his voice sounded distant.

Another *boom* echoed across the night sky. My skin was tingling from the vibration as I crawled along the road, left gasping in the abrupt, extreme quiet. There were no bodies, no evidence at all that anyone else had been here. And then Ambrose dive-bombed me, sending me soaring back into the ditch. I landed hard, and he licked the side of my face. "I'm okay, Ambrose." He only kissed me more, whimpering. I wrapped my arms around him, taking hold of my dragon and never wanting to let go again. "I'm fine. You see? I'm fine."

When he finally flew off me, the breath left my body as I recognized the Vampire King standing in the middle of the road. Killian's guard, alive albeit with gaping wounds, were picking themselves up off the road.

Ari was everything one would expect from the strongest vampire in the world. Tall, solidly built, with a thick beard covering his strong jaw; Ari had been, and still looked like, a Viking, except he wore a tailored suit. That's when it dawned on me. Killian must have called to Ari through their bond— his Sire—requesting assistance. And Ari had wiped the vampires off the face of the earth in a single blast. *Goddess.*

"Killian," Ari said, his voice gruff, and oddly *familiar* after hearing him over the television and radio for years. "Are you all right?"

"I'm not dead yet," Killian grumbled, pushing himself up onto one knee, covered in more wounds than I dared to count. "Thank you for coming."

Relieved, my heart skipped a full beat as he stood, his wounds healing before my eyes.

"It's of no concern," Ari said. "Care to explain what's going on?"

Killian's eyes met mine. "There is someone you need to meet, Sire."

The Vampire King slowly turned to me. A hot rush stormed over me, or maybe that was his dark magic flowing out, making the road hazy as I stared into eyes that were the same shade as mine.

One second, I was crawling on the road. The next, I was lifted to my feet by Ari's hold under my arm, bringing my face directly in front of his widening eyes. "By the Gods, you look exactly like her."

"Like who?" I managed.

"My Zara."

My mother.

I could only gawk as tears fell from the eyes of the most

powerful vampire in the world. Tears for *me*. He slowly set me down, his strong hands cupping my face. "How can this be? How can you be here?"

"Why wouldn't I be here?"

"You died twenty-two years ago."

CHAPTER
Six

THOUGHTS OF VISITING Flora had vanished with Ari's arrival. The last thing I wanted was to bring raging vampires to my aunt's doorstep, and I also didn't want to face another army myself. Killian dismissed his guard to heal their wounds at home, and Ari teleported Killian, Ambrose, and me away from the country road, the wind roaring through the magical veil. When the world came into view again, I had trouble containing my awe. The Manor, grand in size, seemed inconsequential compared to the Citadel. Located on the west bank of the Mississippi River, the plantation stretched over vast, untouched Louisiana countryside. Sitting atop a high hill, the limestone mansion—Greek Revival the same as the Manor—towered over the oak trees surrounding the home. Guards stood at every entrance, every gate, and walked the wrought-iron fence line. Once we entered through the front double doors, Ari led us to a sitting room and took the throne chair. Two servers immediately brought drinks. Two goblets, containing blood.

"Scotch, wine, or water, miss?" the server asked me.

"Wine, please," I replied. "Red, if you have it." In a rush of wind, he left the room and swiftly returned with my wine.

"Thank you." I accepted the glass and took the longest drink of wine, savoring the black-currant flavor on my tongue.

The fire in the massive stone fireplace blazed to life as Killian took a seat in the lion-legged chair near it. Ambrose flew over and curled up in front, falling right to sleep. My heart reached for my sleeping dragon.

"You thought Willa died?" Killian asked, breaking the heavy silence.

Ari finished his drink in one gulp, licking the blood off his lips. "Yes," he answered. He rubbed his eyebrow, moving to stand next to the fireplace. "You died alongside your mother."

My legs shook a little beneath me, so I took a seat in the chair opposite Killian, swallowing more wine. "I was told that my mother died when a rogue vampire slaughtered her."

Ari scrubbed his hand over his face, his mouth down-turned. "That, simply, is untrue." He set the empty goblet on the carved mahogany coffee table. "I am the reason your mother is dead."

My heart plummeted. "But you loved her?"

"Madly," Ari said. Facing the fireplace, the golden light revealed his tension. "When the war between humans and vampires began, I met Zara. We met during peace talks. She, another high priestess, myself, my brother, Ezra … as we were the oldest and strongest vampires leading the war to no longer hide in the shadows. The meeting did not go well. Ezra rejected the idea that vampires and humans could unite. The night I met Zara, my life changed more drastically than when I had been rebirthed." His pained eyes met mine, his smile tender. "One look and I would have given everything I had for a life with her."

Killian asked, "She was your gemina flamma?"

Ari nodded and then looked at the fire again, his arm resting on the mantel. "It did not make sense, not to anyone. No one had ever heard of a vampire bonding with a witch, and there has never been one since, but there was no denying the truth: I would have burned the world to have her, and she me."

I pondered that. "Maybe there would be more bonds if vampires and witches were allowed to interact."

"That's very well correct," Ari agreed. "We bonded within a week of meeting each other in secret, but somehow the Assembly found out." His chin lifted as the wood in the fire popped. "The Assembly stripped Zara of her high-priestess position and banished her from her coven."

I snorted. "That sounds familiar."

Killian's voice was pained as he asked his Sire, "Why did you keep Zara and Willa from me?"

"To protect her, and to protect Willa, we told very few," Ari answered. His eyes shut tight, his voice breaking as he said, "Zara gave up so much for me. I promised that we'd make our world better so one day she could return to her family, her friends, everyone she had to leave behind. That was why I chose to climb the ladder to power. It was not a hunger to rule, but to change the world so Zara didn't have to give anything up." He stared into the flames. "But then everything changed."

"What happened?" I said softly.

Ari opened his eyes, and a blinding smile crossed his face. "Zara became pregnant." But then his smile fell. "We couldn't wait and hope. We needed to improve the world you were about to be born into, immediately. Vampires wouldn't have accepted you, and neither would witches. Zara and I had one shot to make this world safe for you."

I glanced at Killian. He was watching Ari closely, questions swirling in his eyes. Ari had never told him this story, then.

"Back in the early nineteen hundreds, rumors began to whisper on the wind of a dark power hidden near the Black Sea." Ari took the seat across from me, clasping his hands in his lap. "Power that had no beginning and no end. Power so rich that vampires and witches alike searched for it." His eyebrows gathered together. "I hired scouts and trackers to find it, and five days after your fourth birthday, I got word the power had been located. Deep in a cave, guarded by a spell that could only be broken by a powerful witch."

The fire crackled in the hearth, drawing Ari's gaze again. "Plans, you see, can start off with such good intentions. We were at war. Fighting to make peace between humans and vampires and fighting to make peace between vampires and witches. Death flourished. Blood was shed unnecessarily." His pained eyes met mine. "Your mother agreed to break the spell so that I could absorb the power."

That made no sense. Witches did not deal in dark magic. Not *ever*. "Why would she do that?"

"To end the fighting," Ari replied. "To keep vampires and witches safe and show them we can live in harmony. We wanted to bring the two races together, finally bind them as allies. Show both vampires and witches a new way of life, one with possibility and prosperity." He paused. "Most of all, she broke that lock for you."

Pain hit the back of my throat. "Why?"

"Because of prejudice. Because you were not welcome as part vampire and part witch." Every single word was a blow I didn't think I could survive, but Ari continued. "With that rich power flowing through my veins, I could rule vampires, change laws, and no one could stand against me. Because of that power, you and any other mixed supernaturals are now welcomed into vampire society."

But clearly his plan hadn't worked entirely. Witches had *not* eliminated prejudice; they would never accept me again.

Killian asked, "Then what went wrong with your plan, Sire?"

"When Zara broke the lock and I absorbed the power, all seemed well. With the enhanced power, I took out my strongest opponents and rose to the title given to me by others: Vampire King. I forged the treaty with the humans, and your mother and I were focused on persuading the witch world to accept mixed races, to accept peace between witches and vampires, but before we could, the power began to kill me," Ari said, his voice losing steam. "Your mother, my *gemina flamma*, realized we needed to remove some of the power, or it would destroy me. To a place only she and I knew about, we bound the magic to ensure no one could find it. But when she performed the ritual and pulled the magic from me, you heard my screams and thought I was dying." His eyes met mine, his lips trembled. "You were caught in the crossfire of the magic. Your mother shielded you."

The ground dropped from under me, my skin flushing hot. "Are you telling me that I killed her?"

"No, *no*," Ari said, and a moment later, he was on his knees in front of me, gripping my hands. "I killed her. I sought that power. I put Zara in that situation, not you, my sweet Willa."

But the kernel of knowledge was there. My mother had no other choice other than to sacrifice herself to save me. My heart felt like it was breaking, my eyelids becoming gummy, but I wouldn't break down here, not now, not with a thousand questions still rushing through my mind.

My vision blurred as Ari added, "But even after your mother's death, the power I released wasn't enough. That is why I gave more of my power away."

"To who?" I managed to ask.

Killian answered, "The Wardens."

"Indeed," Ari replied, keeping my hands tight in his. And in one wild moment, I realized the Vampire King was kneeling at my feet, pleading for me to understand. "Though being the first I gave the power to, Killian absorbed more. With each gift, the power lessened, only giving as much as was necessary to keep me living."

I noted a sweetness between Killian and Ari. Respect. Friendship. All of that was there, but something *more.* Love.

"I didn't know it, then, but the power did not like being ripped apart; it wanted to stay whole, which was what made your mother's removal of some of it so dangerous."

"What she took when she died was enough to keep the magic from killing you?" I asked.

Ari nodded, scraping a shaking hand through his hair.

"And you thought I'd died with her …"

He nodded.

I glanced down to his other hand covering mine, feeling the tremor run through him. "You lost not only my mother, but you thought you also lost me, all in the same night?"

Tears welled in his eyes. "I did."

"I'm sorry," I managed to choke out.

Ari pulled me into his arms and held me tight. "I am sorry also."

I stayed there, in the safety and warmth of Ari's hold. It felt … *nice.* It felt like something I never had before. When I leaned away, I caught Killian's tender gaze, and after a big, deep breath, Ari took my hands again, like he was scared I was going to vanish.

I was trying to process all this but was failing miserably.

"One thing I don't understand is if my mother threw her shield around me, why did you think I died?"

"The force of the magic ripping from me knocked me out cold," Ari explained, wiping his eyes. "When I woke again, you were gone; your mother was gone, and so was your Ambrose."

I glanced at Ambrose, who snored softly. "He was there too?"

"Ambrose was a present from your mother and me on your fourth birthday, just three months before everything went so wrong," Ari said, regarding Ambrose with amusement. "He was meant to protect you. Though I see he never quite grew as big—or as aggressive—as I hoped."

I smiled at my lazy dragon. "He might be small, but he protected me fiercely tonight."

"Then I am glad you've had him." His finger tucked under my chin, turning my focus back to him. "Where have you lived all these years?"

"With Flora."

Ari's nostrils flared, his lips pulling back, baring his fangs. "Your aunt?"

"Well, to be more precise, I lived with Flora until I went to the Assembly for schooling and came home to live with her during my summers off, but when I failed the Summer Solstice Rite, I was banished from ever working for the Assembly or returning to my coven. I moved to Charleston three years ago and haven't seen her since."

Ari lurched to his feet, his wide eyes, showing the whites. "You mean to tell me Flora stole you away from me that night, hid you in her coven, and then banished you?" His neck corded, his extremities shaking. "I will bleed her dry."

"Don't." I shot up out of my seat and latched on to his arm, imploring him. "Please don't. I need to understand why all of this has happened and why she took me away from you. She'll have answers only she can tell me."

He studied me, then sighed dejectedly, sliding his hand over mine. "If this is what you ask of me, this I can do for you."

"Thank you." I squeezed his hand back before I took my seat again, sipping my wine, trying to piece this together. I examined the vampire who was my father, who watched me intently, like there was nothing in the world he wouldn't give me.

I had family, true family, and maybe, just *maybe*, I would experience love the way I'd always craved, real love. Love that didn't come with strings attached. In a world that once felt very alone, that might never be the case again.

But I didn't know Ari. I didn't remember him as my father, and all I could see when I looked upon him was a stranger. A stranger who'd endangered my life.

"Isn't it weird I don't crave blood? If I'm part vampire, why don't I want to drink blood?"

Killian, who remained in his seat giving Ari and I the time we needed, added, "She also doesn't have magic."

Ari dismissed the remark with a wave of his hand, moving to rest his arm on the fireplace mantel again. "Impossible. You come from two powerful bloodlines. We expected you to be brimming with power when you came of age."

"He's not lying to you," I said to Ari. "It was why the Assembly banished me. I couldn't pass the rite because I don't have a lick of magic to my name."

Ari studied me with a frown, then set that frown on Ambrose. "And he never came into his power either."

The same headache I'd had when I first woke up at the Manor returned, came back tenfold. I drained the rest of my wine, then rubbed my temple. "Yes, there are a million questions and I suspect most of them Flora can answer."

"I agree," Ari said. "However, now that I am involved, I'll have to go through the proper channels to speak with Flora. I will arrange for us to meet with the Assembly."

"For now, Willa should rest," Killian interjected, rising.

Ari nodded. "Yes, it's been a difficult journey. I'll have the staff take you to your room."

I missed home. Gwen. Finnick. My bookshop. "Only a temporary room," I told Ari. "Once this—whatever *this* is—is over, I'm going home to Charleston and back to my life."

Ari clasped his hands together behind him. "Your life is not mine to dictate, even if you are my heir."

My gaze caught Killian's, whose intense stare had never left mine. *Okay, okay, so you were right about him after all.*

As if he heard me, he grinned.

When I turned to Ari again, he arched an eyebrow in Killian's direction. Their eyes glazed over during some private conversation, and Ari eventually nodded, his mouth curving slightly at the corners. "You've got my security in your arsenal now," he said. "Use them. Keep her safe."

"Yes, Sire," Killian said.

"Now, as for you ..." Ari drawled, helping me to my feet. Leaning in, he kissed my one cheek and then the other, and an aching, lonely part of my soul relished the warmth of his affection. "We will get answers," he said, leaning away, his gaze alert. "We will get justice. We will make this world safe for you again so you can return to your life in Charleston. Welcome home, my darling Willa."

CHAPTER
Seven

AFTER SAYING good night to Killian and Ari, the staff led me to my room for the night, with Ambrose flying behind me, and I felt like I'd stepped back into the past: eighteenth-century furniture, a marble fireplace with a blazing fire, a four-poster queen with dark-green linens matching the flowered wallpaper, an assortment of pillows. The room was fitting for an old vampire—grand and over the top—but unease crawled along my skin. I climbed onto the high bed, staring around at what may be my bedroom for Goddess knows how long, and I tried not to give in to my fears as long minutes ticked by.

My emotions felt like they had been ripped out, cut apart, and then reassembled. I had a father again. A real *father.*

No longer was I, Willa Farrington, a magic-less witch without a coven.

In fact, I was Willa von Stein, daughter of the Vampire King.

I tried to absorb that, accept that, deal with *that*, but failed miserably.

So much had happened. Too much. I needed to find my grounding again. Ambrose parked his butt on the end of the bed as I dug my cell phone out of my back pocket and texted Finnick: BRING GWEN, I NEED YOU BOTH.

In a blink of an eye, my best friends stood before me.

"Thank you for coming—"

A loud *bang* startled me, followed by Gwen's gasp and a deep grunt, and then I realized I'd made a grave mistake.

"Stop," I screamed, lurching off the bed. Gwen and Finnick were pressed against the wall, their legs dangling a foot off the ground, a shirtless Killian's hand on each of their necks. I rushed forward, placing my hand on his back, his flexed muscles quivering. "Let them go. They're my friends. I called them here."

His fingers only tightened; Gwen and Finnick remaining motionless.

"Killian," I said gently, sliding my hand down his arm, only now feeling the coolness of his flesh, but his power felt hot against my skin, tingling along my fingertips. I might have lost myself in the pulsating sensation if I didn't see Gwen's wide eyes. "Put them down. Now."

Killian's back muscles twitched, the hardness of his muscles beneath my hand softening. He put Gwen and Finnick back on their feet, their attention on their Warden, who turned to me.

It took every bit of strength I had not to gape at his flaw-less body, screaming powerful masculinity. Every line of Killian was taut, vibrating with his magic. Suddenly all I could see were his sculpted, kissable lips, and wondered how he would taste. I fought the urge to run my hands over his wide shoulders, down to his squared chest, over each dip and curve of his abdomen, to the V at his waist. Would he groan if I kissed him there? Shiver? Holy Goddess, he was perfection. My tummy tightened against the need flooding me and I met his eyes. They glowed bright sliver, intensity simmering, shining with promise.

Killian blinked, the emotions on his face locking up tight. "Next time, please notify me of any guests."

"I will, promise," I said, willing the heat pulsing between us to settle. "I'm sorry. I wasn't thinking."

The dip of his chin was his only response before heading out of the bedroom, shutting the door behind him.

"Spill. The. Details," Finnick purred, pointing to the door Killian had gone out. He mouthed to keep the conversation private, *"You slept with him, didn't you?"*

"No, I did not," I mouthed back. We'd all gotten very good at reading lips over the years.

Finnick's brows shot up. *"That vampire nearly ripped off my head. He wants you."*

I felt the blush rising to my face and tried to find a snappy response, but I couldn't come up with one. The physical attraction to Killian had always been there, but this was ... deeper, *needier*. The truth was, I wanted to get to know him more, and I wanted him to know me too. There was a pull between us that I couldn't ignore. The desire pulsated like a living thing, making me ... hungry for just a taste.

I eventually shrugged. *"Something seems to be brewing there."*

Gwen grinned devilishly, and mouthed, *"Good. He's hot, and he'll keep you safe."*

"And the desire you two gave off is ..." Finnick fanned himself.

"Ew. Can we not talk about my desire, please?"

Finnick laughed. "Yes," he said aloud. "But he passes the vibe check, so you've got our full approval." With a wink, he moved to the bed, sitting next to Ambrose, who was watching them with little worry.

I sat against the pillows, Gwen on the other side of me, and asked, "Obviously a lot has happened since we're"—she glanced around the room, her nose scrunched—"are we at the Manor?"

"The Citadel," I corrected her.

If my best friends could have paled, they would have.

"Damn, Willa," Finnick drawled, shaking his head slowly. "I'm with Killian on this one. Next time, please text—I need you, but I'm at the Citadel. It's a major no-no to just pop into the Vampire King's house unannounced."

"It's not when he's my father," I said.

Finnick blinked. "Tell. Us. Everything."

So, I did. I let the words flow and verbally vomited everything that had happened since the Blood Moon Festival, which felt like a lifetime ago.

By the time I finished, Gwen's expression mirrored my pain. "Your mother died saving you?"

"I guess, yeah," I replied, picking at the blanket beneath me. "And I'm …" I breathed through the misery squeezing my throat, and in the safety of my best friends, I let the tears fall. "How different would everything have been had I not run into the magic? My mother would be alive. I would have … I would have been understood. I would have felt I like I belonged every single day of my life."

Gwen placed a hand on my thigh. "Don't do that to yourself. Sometimes bad shit happens. You were a loving daughter and thought your father was being hurt, and your mother was just loving you back the same way. Whatever happened that night is not your fault, Willa."

I wiped the moisture off my face. "Maybe not, but it doesn't change that fact that I am here, and she is not."

Finnick sighed, a very human thing. "Do you have any idea why your aunt would lie to you about what happened to your mother?"

I'd told Gwen and Finnick everything from my past. We had no secrets. "I don't know the reason." But then I mouthed in case anyone was listening, *"But I'm wary because of it. What if Flora didn't tell me because she didn't want me to find Ari? What if he's the danger here?"*

Finnick immediately shook his head. "Impossible," he said aloud.

Gwen shrugged and mouthed, *"I'm with Finnick. Ari is good and kind, and he's not a threat to you."*

"It feels that way to me too, but I don't know what to believe anymore." I paused and sighed, saying aloud, not caring who heard me, "I have no idea how to see myself anymore. I'm not the witch I thought I was. I don't know who I am now."

Finnick examined me, then gave his classic smart-ass smile. "The way I see it, this isn't so bad. First, you belong to the most powerful bloodline in the United States. You're basically royalty, Willa. And second, who cares if you're part vampire? Vampires rule. What's the big deal?"

"You two rule," I agreed with a nod before my heart twisted. "The big deal is I can't ever go back to my coven now. Or any coven, for that matter. They will never accept me."

Gwen frowned. "That's hard, for sure, but you also have what you never had before—your father."

"Even if I'm confused, I am glad that he's back in my life," I said.

Finnick asked, "What are the chances your aunt didn't know you were part vampire?"

"I don't see how she couldn't have known, but I wonder if she didn't tell me to keep me safe and to keep me in the coven. Who knows her reasoning, but you both know, once word leaks that Ari has a daughter who is part witch, every witch will turn their nose down at me."

Finnick cocked his head, fire in his eyes. "I'm not sure I'm getting why you care so much what those stuffy witches think. Not only did those bitches already banish you, but I thought you liked it in Charleston."

"I love Charleston," I agreed. "I love my bookshop and my life with you both, but my coven, and the Assembly, were home for a long time. I have friends there, my aunt." So many witches I left behind. Even Mikkel, who I hadn't seen since he ended things, was in so many of my memories. It felt impossibly hard to even imagine I would never see any of them again. It felt … *wrong.* "I might not want to live there again, but now, I won't even be allowed to visit."

"Those rules are stupid," Gwen snapped.

"They are," I agreed. They only validated my parents' intentions. At one time, I wouldn't have been able to live in Charleston among the vampires. Their sacrifice had allowed for that. If Ari hadn't absorbed the power and become Vampire King, I would have been banished to live among humans. "And now it's like, where do I even belong? I'm not quite witch, not quite vampire. Everything is upside down. My entire life is a lie. I don't know who I am, or who to trust, or what story is real."

Gwen took my hands in hers, squeezing tight. "You're Willa, and that's all that matters, and we love you."

Finnick agreed with a nod. "Everything will sort itself out. Ari and Killian will stop these attacks on you. You are exactly where you should be to stay safe. You'll get answers to all these questions, and life will settle again. You'll still be you. You'll still have your bookshop. And you'll still have us."

I couldn't help but smile. "That is all very much true, and I love you."

Gwen pressed a quick kiss to my cheek. "Besides, maybe that's why you felt so comfortable in Charleston. I mean, you are the only witch to ever move into town. Every other banished witch has chosen to live with humans, but not you."

At that, my mind stuttered. "You know, I hadn't ever thought of that, but you're right."

Gwen nodded like she was onto something. "My guess is you always felt like you belonged in Charleston because in your heart you knew you were meant to be among vampires."

"Maybe," I said, a lump in my throat.

"So, the way I see it," Gwen continued, her eyes twinkling, "witches got you first, but now it's time for you to live among your other nature. To be, and to live, as a vampire."

And just like that, I felt as if a weight had been lifted off me. "Thank you for coming. Really. You have no idea how much I needed this. I love you both so much."

"Love you back, vampy-witchy." Finnick grinned.

I lifted my eyebrows. "What? No more, witchy-witchy?"

"Nah." Finnick waved and winked. "That was so last year."

I laughed, leaning forward and fell into their open arms. I couldn't ask for better friends, and never for single second, would I ever forget how lucky I was to have them.

The antique bed groaned beneath us. "All of this is going to be a huge adjustment," I said. "I mean, look at this room. It's like I stepped into the eighteenth century. I don't belong here."

"Maybe you do," Gwen offered. "You just didn't know it."

I had a hard time wrapping my head around that. "Maybe you're right." I heaved a long sigh, forcing myself not to get too ahead of myself. I would take it one night at a time until my life made sense again. Until I stopped being in danger. "Maybe things never felt good, settled, happy, because I only knew half of myself. Maybe being here, with Ari, is the part that's always been missing. Maybe this is the best thing that's ever happened to me."

Finnick's smile beamed. "And there's our gorgeous, full-of-sunshine Willa."

"As stunningly bright as ever," Gwen agreed with a nod.

I laughed and then kept laughing for another hour while my best friends made life feel somewhat normal.

After we said our goodbyes, and they vanished from the room, Ambrose woke up with a big yawn and crawled onto my lap, rubbing his wet nose against my cheek. "I'm sorry this has been so exhausting, buddy, but we'll be okay. Promise." His soft purr was interrupted by a knock on the door. "Come in."

Killian, now wearing a black T-shirt, opened the door slightly. He stared at me for a long moment. "I'm sorry if I frightened you earlier."

"You didn't frighten me," I said. *I wanted to explore the rest of your bare flesh that I couldn't see.* I swore silver flashed through his eyes at my salacious thought. "But I think Gwen and Finnick might have died for a second time."

His mouth twitched. "If you need me, I'm in the room across from yours. You're safe to sleep tonight."

Goddess, how he could melt my bones and my insides all at once was a gift I'd never received before. "I think your ninja moves earlier proved that well enough."

He chuckled, low and deep. "Sleep well, Willa." He began to shut the door but then suddenly opened it. "I understand learning your vampire heritage is unsettling, and it is understandable to miss your life in your coven, but perhaps instead of sadness, you might consider feeling angry for how they turned their backs on you." His smoky eyes flared with power. "How they abandoned you. How they have not contacted you since you left them." Though his voice softened, his expression did not. "Your life has changed now, that is for certain. Will you mourn what you've lost? Yes. But you moved to Charleston for a reason, were accepted by Charleston's vampires, even when they thought you were only a witch. Yes, vampires are attacking you now, but they're also protecting you."

I pulled the bedspread and then stopped as things became clear. Vampires had never let me down, but witches had.

"From the ashes of what you thought was important, a new life will be reborn. A new purpose. A new path." He hesitated. The air charging between us sizzled against my skin. "You will be all right, Willa. You will be kept safe until we find out why you're being hunted. And when I find those hunting you, revenge will be ours."

He shut the door behind him with a click.

I caught Ambrose damn near smiling after Killian.

"You like him, huh?" I asked my dragon, not caring if Killian heard me. I kissed Ambrose's warm head, staring at the door Killian just closed. "Yeah, buddy, so do I."

CHAPTER
Eight

THE NEXT NIGHT, after a long, deep sleep, I woke to a soft knock and breakfast for Ambrose and me waiting outside the bedroom door. My witch side still needed a good eight hours of sleep to function, even if my vampire side only needed a few hours. We both ate quickly and, back in bed again, I drank two coffees before I found the energy to head into the shower. I took my time, letting the hot water wash over me, while Ambrose splashed in the claw-foot bathtub. When I got out, I wrapped myself in a towel, dried my hair, and put on light makeup to hide the dark circles under my eyes.

When I returned to the bedroom, I halted, hardly believing my eyes. Ambrose flew ahead of me, landing on the bed's linen-gray duvet. Every antique piece of furniture had been removed, replaced by a contemporary walnut bed frame, with matching double dresser and vanity set. Even the long curtains had been replaced with striped cotton ones.

I saw a note on the bedside table next to the gold metallic lamp, and my breath left me in a rush when I read the beautiful script handwriting: I HOPE THIS FEELS A LITTLE MORE LIKE HOME. KILLIAN.

He didn't. He couldn't have…?

He most certainly did redecorate the bedroom, obviously having heard my conversation with Gwen and Finnick about my not feeling like I belonged there. Overwhelmed by his kindness, I quickly dressed in jeans and a black silk blouse. I said to my dragon, "Come on, Ambrose, we've got things to do."

He yipped at me, following me out to the hallway. Killian's bedroom door was open, indicating he'd already started his night. To the guard on the right of my door, I asked, "Is Killian around?"

"He's in meetings with the King, Ms. Farrington," the guard said. "Do you need him immediately?"

I got the sense if I said yes that he'd interrupt them. "No, no, it's fine," I said. "Did he leave any instructions for me?"

"No, ma'am," he said.

I nibbled my lip. "Would it be all right if I went down to the kitchen?"

The guards exchanged a long look before the one said, "The Citadel is your home now, Ms. Farrington. You do not need to ask permission to do anything. Follow the hallway, the kitchen will be on the right."

Damn. Word had spread fast. Ari's daughter. I almost powered up my cell phone, but I didn't need to. This news would already be headlining every top supernatural media outlet.

"Oh," I said. "Well, thank you."

He simply nodded.

Feeling like there were eyes on me everywhere, I quickly made my way down the hallway and onto the lower level. I supposed being Ari's daughter, the guards would look at this as my house, and that they had some obligation to me, but I didn't feel that way.

When I entered the kitchen, I found a vampire cooking at the stove. "Hi," I announced.

A quick glance over her shoulder, her eyes widened. "Oh, hello, mistress, what can I get for you?"

"It's Willa," I corrected her, stepping into the kitchen, with Ambrose fluttering next to me. "Actually, I was wondering if it's possible for me to take over the kitchen for the next couple hours so I could cook something."

She blinked. "Yes, of course, Mistress Willa. The pantry is stocked. Help yourself to anything." She stirred whatever was in the pot on the stove before putting a lid on it. "The stew for dinner tonight needs to simmer awhile anyway. Enjoy yourself. I'll make sure no one interrupts you."

"Thanks," I said with a smile. "And again, it's just Willa."

She gave a nod but stayed silent. I fed Ambrose some cooked chicken from the fridge after nuking it and then I hurried to the pantry and fridge, finding all the makings for Italian sausage pasta. Taking out my phone, I hit my playlist, and Ed Sheeran's smooth voice filled the air, and I fell into the happy rhythm of cooking, something that always relaxed me.

By the time the meal was finished, the kitchen smelled of Italian spices. Not quite knowing what to do next, I said to absolutely no one, "Um, hello, can someone help me?"

The vampire who served me my wine last night was before me by the next blink of my eyes. "Yes, mistress?"

"Willa is fine," I said. "What's your name?"

"Raphael, mistress."

He must have been turned in his late teens because he still had a baby face. The black and white suit he wore looked dashing on him, distinguished, leading me to believe that he'd been rebirthed during the Victorian era. He held that classy air about him reminiscent of old vampires sometimes. "Hi, Raphael, it's good to meet you."

I received a genuine smile. "It's nice to meet you too. What can I do for you?"

"Do you mind asking Killian to meet me down here, and … um … can we have some privacy?"

"Of course." Raphael was gone before my next breath.

Then I heard footsteps coming down the staircase. I turned back to the stove and stirred the pasta, expecting nerves that never came.

Energy flowed throughout the room seconds before Killian asked, "What's this?"

I glanced over my shoulder. He was leaning against the doorway, his head tilted to the side, Ambrose circling his legs. Killian bent to give him a pat on his head.

"Lunch," I told him.

He raised an eyebrow. "For?"

"You," I said, using the wooden spoon in my hand to point at a stool at the island. "You've saved my life a couple times now, figured the least I could do is make you lunch."

He revealed nothing as he took a seat on the stool. Leaning forward, he sniffed the plate of pasta I'd already served up. "You added blood?"

"Of course." I scooped more pasta to my plate, without the blood. "I've learned from Gwen and Finnick that not adding blood to a vampire's meal is rude."

He cracked a smile. Maybe the first real smile I'd ever seen on his face, and my heart skipped a full beat. Goddess, Dracula had nothing on this vampire—humans would offer their willing necks with little fight. Hell, I wanted to offer mine as I sat next to him.

He opened the bottle of red wine and began pouring my glass. "What spurred this invitation?" he asked.

I smoothed the napkin over my lap. "A few things, but also as a thank-you for redecorating my room to make me more comfortable."

He poured his glass. "You don't need to thank me."

I reached out before second-guessing myself and gripped his powerful forearm. Electricity hummed from his flesh to mine, and he stiffened. "I did need to thank you for that," I replied. "You haven't needed to do anything that you have for me, and I want you to know that I'm grateful. Truly."

He looked at where my hand touched him, and suddenly my skin tingled, the heat burning that spot, pooling far lower in my body. When his glowing eyes met mine again, he murmured, "All of this can't be easy on you. To make you more comfortable is the least I can do."

"Which is very considerate." I forced myself to remove my hand, picking up my glass, and sipping the wine. "Can I ask you a question?"

He nodded, picking up his fork. "You can."

But I may not answer was implied.

I set my wineglass back on the island. "Who are you, exactly?"

He halted with his fork halfway to his mouth. "Is this a trick question?"

"When I first met you, you were a stern vampire who looked like you couldn't form a smile if you tried. Everything I've heard about you is nothing like the vampire sitting next to me."

He ate a forkful of pasta. "I'm myself with Ari and a few other Wardens who are close friends."

I tested the pasta, proud of the explosion of flavors. "But no one else?"

"No."

I paused. "But you're showing me this side of yourself."

His gaze held mine. "I am."

"You want me to know you, then?"

A nod.

"Then tell me everything about you."

"From the very beginning?"

"Well, I already know your rebirth story," I said, sticking my fork into a piece of sausage. "Tell me more about your fiancée."

He took a long sip of his wine before answering. "Her

name was Anna May. She was a sweet farmer's daughter to whom I proposed marriage."

The pain in his voice had me pushing around the pasta on my plate. "You didn't go back and see her after you were turned?"

He shook his head, stabbing the pasta on his plate. Before he shoved it into his mouth, he added, "But I did learn from the newspaper that she married a few months after I had been declared dead."

"I guess that's good."

"It is," he agreed with a nod. "She was a lovely girl. I suspect I would have had a very happy life with her."

I shook my head slowly. "I can't imagine being forced to walk away from happiness. That must have been hard."

"It's been a very long time. Pain eases over the years."

"I suppose that's true," I said, glancing down at Ambrose who sat on his butt, his tongue wagging out the side of his mouth, waiting for me to either drop food or get suckered into feeding him. I took a piece of sausage off my plate then offered it to him before turning to Killian again. "So, after you walked away from the life you knew, you joined Ari's ranks?"

He gave a brief nod. "When he left the human military behind to bring vampires out of the shadows and solidify peace with humans, I agreed with what he fought for. I'd seen war. It benefits no one. I wanted an end to the violence."

I regarded this curious vampire.

He laughed. The first time I'd heard him do that. "Why are you looking at me like that?"

"Oh," I said, my heartbeat quickening as I leaned forward, closing the distance between us, "I'm just thinking that behind all those hard muscles and sharp fangs, you're just a really good guy, huh?"

"In some eyes, maybe. In others, I suspect not." He turned to his pasta and continued to eat, so I did the same, finishing lunch in a comfortable silence, decidedly certain that the vampire next to me was as good as they come.

After Killian cleared the dishes, we cleaned up together to the horror of the kitchen staff, who Killian firmly sent away when they wouldn't accept that I wanted to wash my own dishes.

As I set the last dish in the cupboard, Killian said, "Thank you for tonight. It's been a long time since I've done this."

"Had lunch with someone?" I asked with a snort, shutting the cupboard door, turning to face him.

Energy pulsed like a heartbeat, causing my nipples to pucker as he took a step closer. "Had a meal with a woman."

I swallowed against the way his voice lowered at *woman* and how those two syllables stormed through my blood. I inhaled sharply, his wintery pine aroma overwhelming my senses. "You're welcome. I enjoyed myself too."

The silvering of his eyes told me I was failing miserably at hiding the excitement building inside me. He closed the remaining distance between us slowly, letting me watch every powerful step he took. His hand came to my arm, and that intentional touch kicked up my heart rate even more. Suddenly everything between us became charged, damn near electrified. His presence was all around me, his power washing over me, his mouth close to mine.

Aware of my desire, his nostrils flared, as he brushed a soft kiss against my cheek. The world stopped spinning as the air left my lungs in a rush, and my head turned without so much as a thought, only a pure desperation to feel him against my flesh.

Except, before my lips met his, he pulled away.

His glowing eyes were dancing. "Thank you again."

As he strode away, and feeling like he suddenly had one up on me, I shoved all my desire, all my drenched, aching need into the air, letting him scent *that*.

He stiffened at the doorway, glancing back. His bright,

glowing eyes, paired with the ravenous hunger on his face, nearly melted the panties off my body. "Are you prepared to finish what you're starting?"

"Oh, are we starting something?" I asked, striding up to him. He went ramrod stiff as I molded myself to his body, leaning against the hefty erection at my stomach. "Aren't we just saying goodbye?"

His chest rumbled.

Having the upper hand again, I grinned and meant to walk out of the door, except that a blast of wind slammed the door shut. Killian pressed me against the wall, his hard muscles a shield I never wanted gone. His hands braced my face, his lips inches from mine. Eyes glowing, he murmured, "You know we're starting something."

"Maybe I do."

The air was on fire between us, electricity pinging as he brought his mouth closer, enough to smell Italian spices on the tongue I craved to taste. "If I kiss you, Willa, there is no walking away for me." His gaze swept over my lips before meeting my eyes.

My head was spinning at the feel of his hands on me—at the power in the air around us. I could feel *him* entering every molecule of my body. His icy, woodsy aroma enveloping me. His touch burning me. His passion searing along my skin. It was like I knew all of Killian without knowing him. I didn't question if I should let this happen, I *knew* it had to. I threaded my hands into his hair and brought his mouth to mine.

He groaned against my lips, and I echoed the sound, parting my mouth, allowing his tongue entrance. I moaned as I tasted him, and he grunted for all the same reasons, his hands exploring my body like he needed to learn it, to feel my curves. I dragged my hands from his hair to his strong shoulders down to his rippling arm muscles.

Until Killian broke the kiss, leaving me breathless after hearing a soft knock on the door. "Go away," he growled.

"I'm sorry to interrupt," Raphael said from the doorway. "But Ari requests your presence in the library."

"Thank you," I breathed, desperately trying to get control of my tingling nerve endings.

Killian waited for Raphael to leave before he set that smoldering stare on me, cupping my face, and cursed. "We need to go."

I saw the question there. All it would take was for me to say: *I need you now,* and we'd be late to meet Ari …

CHAPTER
Nine

WHEN WE WALKED into the library, I moved toward the bookshelf, dragging my fingers against the leathery spines of the books, fighting against reining in my wicked thoughts. Killian silently followed, settling in near the fireplace, and his scent carried to me, tempting me to turn around and finish what we started. Goddess, his kiss still lingered on my lips. I brushed my fingers there, feeling the tingling of his touch.

A low groan broke the silence. "It would be wise to stop thinking about whatever you're thinking about before your father gets here," Killian murmured.

I glanced over my shoulder. "Maybe next time don't kiss me like that, and we won't be in this situation."

His nostrils flared, his eyes glowing. "That is a promise I will break."

My stomach somersaulted under the assault of this raging passion, when I heard voices coming down the hallway. Killian chuckled as I turned back to the books and began thinking about cleaning a dirty toilet.

"Good, you're both here," Ari announced, entering the library, looking handsome and prominent, wearing a suit with a black tie.

He didn't seem to notice the desire hanging thickly in the air or didn't react to it if he did. "News from the Assembly?" I asked, moving closer, near the fireplace.

"Indeed," said Ari. "We have an audience with them."

Nerves raced up my spine, but I swallowed, shoving them away. To visit the Assembly meant to go before the five most powerful witches in the United States, the very witches who banished me. How would they react to my being part vampire? While I was desperate to get answers from my aunt, I was about to walk into a place where I'd be stripped of defenses and exposed to their judgment.

"I assume you want to come along," Ari said to Killian.

He nodded. "Yes, Sire."

Ari paused to examine me, and then he said softly, "Your aunt will answer for her deceit. However, I am aware that facing her now, knowing the truth and revealing this truth to the high priestesses who banished you may be difficult for you."

Part of me wanted to stay back, to not face the truth that my aunt had lied to me my entire life and had stolen my heritage from me. But Killian's words to me yesterday still echoed in my mind, and the other part of myself—the stronger part—wanted to face them, show them that they could never break me.

Killian's fingers slid into mine, and I looked up into his eyes. "Together," he said, giving a curt nod. "We will face them *together*."

"Not only face them, Willa," Ari added. "We will show them exactly where you always belonged."

Everything suddenly seemed so simple … and good. For so long I struggled to find the place I fit in, but now I knew why, *here* was where I belonged. With my father, and my mother had she been here too. I didn't belong in the Assembly's world where someone like me wasn't accepted. I belonged in this new world my parents had forged. I squeezed Killian's hand. It felt right being next to Killian too. "All right, let's go."

I caught the pride in Killian's smile before Ari took my other hand. Wind and darkness whipped around me like a safe tornado rushing around me, until I spotted the Assembly's old stone mansion, with the river running behind it, the grounds on the right an extensive garden for herbs. To the left, a lush botanical garden, where witches read and studied, surrounded by the gifts of Mother Nature. Originally, the mansion had been built as an all-girls school. When witches came out to the world, the Assembly bought the property, and through magic they restored the decrepit building, bringing back its original beauty. *Home.*

"Are you all right?" Killian asked.

From the age of six, I'd spent ten months at the Assembly every year for schooling, returning to Flora's during the summer months off. But as Killian had said it, these witches turned their backs on me. I nodded. "This was home for a very long time."

"Until it wasn't," Killian said, ire lacing his voice.

Ari just scowled at the house.

Obviously expecting us, we were greeted by three witches with defensive magic who led us—one walking ahead and two behind—into the bowels of the mansion. I couldn't hear any young witches but wondered if Ari and Killian could. Neither spoke along the way, Ari in front of me, Killian behind, a strong, impenetrable shield. The curved staircase led to an all-stone room the Assembly called Conclave, where the high priestesses sat at a long table. Radiant light came from wall sconces around the room; a fire in the fireplace brought warmth into the space. From the Northeast region, Esmeralda. Sybil from the West. Beatrix from the Southwest. And Helena from the Midwest. But no Aunt Flora …

Three of the high priestesses were strangers to me, beyond seeing them at galas and when they banished me.

Esmeralda was Mikkel's mother, and at one point in my life, before the rite, I thought she'd become my mother through bonding.

Gentle and wise, Esmeralda's green eyes held mine when we stopped in front of the table. With Killian and Ari on either side of me, Ari got right to the point. "Were you all aware Willa is part vampire and from my bloodline?" he asked.

The high priestesses exchanged wide-eyed looks. "This is news to us," Helena said, her lip curling. "We only met Willa when she came to live with Flora after the death of Zara."

Of course. The Assembly knew nothing of me; my parents made sure of it. They had kept me hidden, a secret. But Flora *must* have known.

"Then let me declare it now." Ice laced Ari's voice. "Willa Farrington is my heir."

Four sets of eyes turned to me.

"An heir I thought had died alongside her mother. Only to find out that Flora took my daughter and lied to me about her death." His nostrils flared, fangs bared. "Give Flora to me now so she may answer for her crimes."

A long sigh fell from Esmeralda's lips, her fingers laced together on top of the table. "If the crime is true, then yes, Flora will need to answer for it, but I'm afraid we do not know where she is."

My heart took a direct hit. I needed to know the truth, I wouldn't jump to conclusions. My aunt had been loving to me after my mother's passing. Banishing me from the Assembly, and my coven, wasn't easy for her, but she'd had no choice. "She's missing?" I asked.

Esmeralda gave a brief nod. "She has been gone for four days now. We've tried locating her but have been unsuccessful."

Killian's thoughts were written all over his face. "She wouldn't hurt me," I said, more to myself than him.

From her seat, Sybil twirled her blonde hair around her finger and asked, "Why do you say that?"

Killian set his intense gaze on the Assembly. "Willa has been targeted this last week. Twice now she's been attacked. Someone has been trying to abduct her."

Helena's brows raised over her dark eyes. "You have not found out the cause?"

I slowly shook my head. "But I know for certain it cannot be Flora behind these attacks. She might have her reasons for keeping me secret from my father, but she would never have others attack me. How could it possibly serve her to abduct me?"

"She has abducted you before," Killian offered gently, brushing his fingers against mine. "Perhaps the same reason is driving her now."

The room sank into heavy silence.

Finally, Beatrix said, "Let us talk a moment."

Ari inclined his head.

With a roar of magic and power, a shield surrounded the witches, flickering like gasoline on water. The witches' mouths moved, some more passionate than others over what-ever they were discussing. I narrowed my eyes to read their mouths.

"They are talking about you," Ari said to my unasked question.

I turned to gape at him. "You can hear them?"

"Yes," he said, his mouth twitching. "But I suspect they do not know that."

Killian chuckled.

I stared at my father, momentarily forgetting all else. His power ... I'd never seen anyone strong enough to break through a high priestess shield. "Is what they're saying in my favor?"

Ari paused, tilting his head. He eventually said, "Esmeralda is on your side."

Then the shield began to fall.

"Willa," Esmeralda said when the shield vanished completely, "the Assembly has decided it is in all our interests to discover who is behind these attacks on you. If you are willing, we can touch your memories and see who is wishing you harm. If this is Flora, we offer our assistance in finding her and bringing her to justice."

I rubbed my arms against the chill in my bones. Witches' justice was no better than vampires'. "What will happen to Flora if it is her?"

Esmeralda smiled tenderly. "It is generous of you to worry over an aunt who has wronged you so gravely, but if she has arranged attacks on you, she will meet her end."

I glanced sidelong at Killian, who slipped my hand in his.

"The truth is the only way back to your life, Willa," he said.

"I know," I said, my stomach quivering. But I forced the unease away—I did not choose this path, and if Flora did, then her choices belonged to her. Stepping out of Killian's hold, I said, "Yes, please touch on my memories, so we can get the answers we need."

The high priestesses rose and came toward us, one by one. I moved to the center of the room, and they circled around me, while Ari and Killian kept close. Power began pulsating like a heartbeat as their magic swept into the circle, the hairs on the back of my neck rising. One high priestess was strong. Four of them together nearly sent me to my knees. The air thrummed with energy like water rushing over me. Until the sensation grew hotter, and steam began filling the air around me, when suddenly I heard voices that did not belong to anyone in the room.

Turning, the steam above me was of my memory when the vampire came into my bookshop and caught my scent. The vampire's face shimmered, going blurry, until he was talking to another vampire. And another. And a few more after that.

Until the witches pulled on the last memory where the intent to harm was first created, and when the thin face, full of hard lines appeared.

Killian and Ari cursed in unison.

"There is your answer, Willa," Esmeralda said as the steam vanished. "The vampire wishing you harm is Ezra von Stein."

CHAPTER
Ten

ARI HAD TELEPORTED us back to the Citadel's command center and was barking out orders the second we arrived, to the surprise of the vampires working behind their desks, who went from zero to a hundred in a blink of an eye.

Standing off to the side of the vampires blurring around me, Killian nudged my elbow, his magic tingling up my arm. "Talk to me."

I considered not saying anything at all, since nothing in a room full of vampires was private, but my head was spinning. "I'm okay," I said, believing that. "I'm just processing all of this and what it means for me."

His lips pressed together in a slight grimace. "It's a lot to process."

I agreed with a nod, rubbing my arms, bringing heat back into my body. "This has been an emotional roller coaster. I don't know what's true, what's not, and why all this is happening."

Killian wrapped an arm around me, tugging me into him. "This, *us*, is true. Believe in that."

I let him fold me into his body, his strong arms like armor that no one could get through.

"Ezra is in New Orleans," a vampire squeaked from behind his desk.

"Do you know his exact location?" Killian asked, releasing me to settle in behind the vamp's chair, folding his arms.

The vamp's fingers moved swiftly across the keyboard until one monitor showed Ezra on the screen. "Earlier tonight, he was in the Garden District, coming out of a house in the heart of the city." More blurring of his fingers, other angles of the street flashed up on the monitors before fading just as fast. "I'm not seeing him on any other cameras in the area."

"Keep scanning," Ari barked from the doorway.

Killian frowned at his Sire, then said to the vampire at his desk, "What information do you have on the house he was at?"

The vampire's fingers clicked again, bringing up a photograph of a beautiful woman. Her long black hair curtained a delicate, pale face, round green eyes, and high cheekbones. "The house belongs to Aurora Dashkov."

"Ezra's lover," Ari explained with a bite to his voice. He glared at the monitor, and if looks could kill, that monitor would be toast. "Aurora is a very old vampire Ezra aligned himself with years ago, no doubt for her power."

"Keep an eye on her," Killian said. "He will return to her."

I stepped in next to Killian and asked the vampire, "Will you search for the High Priestess Flora, too, please?"

Every vampire turned to me.

"Yes, Mistress Willa," the vampire behind his desk said. "I am Darick, and I will do my best to locate your aunt."

"Thank you, Darick," I said. "It's nice to meet you, but please call me Willa."

At a nod from Ari, Darick addressed me again. "Yes, of course, Willa," he said.

"Bring me a report once you have it," Ari ordered. To Killian and me, he added, with a much softer voice, "Come, we could all use a drink."

In full agreement, we followed Ari up to the main level, and entered the library. They both opted for a large glass of scotch, and this time, so did I.

Standing near the antique bar cart, looking as imposing as ever, and after taking a long draw of his drink, Ari said, "It must come as a relief that it is not your aunt behind this attack."

"It is a relief," I admitted, taking the seat near the fireplace. But I wasn't settled, nowhere near it. "But what if Ezra has taken Flora to bait me?"

Killian sat in the seat opposite me, resting his glass, half full of scotch, on his knee. "It's a valid concern."

"Gwen," I exclaimed, shooting up, spilling some of the drink on my hand. "Finnick. What if they're next? Can you get them here to keep them safe?"

"Of course." Ari's eyes went distant. When they cleared, he said, "I've got someone on their way to get your friends."

"Thank you," I breathed, returning to my seat, pounding back more of the oaky scotch.

When I lowered my glass, Killian asked, "If Gwen comes here, what are you going to do about your bookshop?"

"It'll have to stay closed for the time being." I swirled the ice and it clinked against the glass. "Right now, keeping everyone safe is my priority." Because Ezra wasn't only a vampire, he was a vampire with a legion of vampires behind him, and apparently, for whatever reason, he wanted me.

"Excuse me," Raphael said, suddenly popping his head in. "Ambrose wanted to see you."

My dragon nearly choked himself on his leash, and I opened my arms as he flew right onto my lap, kissing my nose. "Missed you, too, buddy." I asked Raphael, "Was he good for you?"

"Yes, Mistress Willa. He had a big dinner and went for a fly."

"Thank you," I said. "And again, it's just *Willa*."

Raphael looked to Ari, and at Ari's nod, he finally relented. "Enjoy the rest of your evening, Willa."

He turned away, and I called after him, "You too."

When I looked back at Ari, he was smiling at me. "You're turning my vampires' worlds upside down."

Regardless of the danger ahead, I still had it in me to smile. "Well, my world has been turned upside down, too, so we're even."

"Fair point." Ari tipped his glass at me before polishing off his drink and then pouring himself another.

Ambrose finally settled, and I took another sip, savoring the deep burn in my dry throat, warming all the cold spots. I went to pet Ambrose, but he jumped off my lap and settled near Killian's feet, who gave the beast a long stroke. Ambrose and me were a package deal, and it touched me that Ambrose liked him so much. "All right," I said, gathering my runaway thoughts. "Can you please explain to me why my uncle is hunting me?"

Ari scrubbed a hand across his face, taking the chair opposite me. The fire lit when he sat down. "Ezra hungers for control. He has ever since we were both turned."

"You were turned together?" I asked.

Ari's gaze went distant, looking at another time, another place. "Yes, by a vampire we met in the forest one evening when we were collecting wood for our father. Celeste was lonely, alone for far too long. We both fell under her charming spell, and when she offered us immortality, we took it."

I sipped my drink, relishing the burn in my throat. "I take it since she's not with you now, something happened to her."

"When Celeste and I grew closer, Ezra killed her," Ari said flatly, lost in his memories, staring into the fire. Until he blinked, his gaze clearing to me sitting across from him. "If he could not have her, no one could have her."

"Wow. Asshole, much? Was that the beginning of the rift between you and your brother?"

Ari nodded. "There had always been a friendly competition between us growing up. But things began to change when, as new vampires, it became obvious Celeste and I were falling in love."

I glanced at Killian then, finding his gaze on me, not his Sire. Trying to decide what was worse: having a toxic family or not having one at all, I asked Ari, "Did you and Ezra part ways after Celeste, then?"

Ari leaned back in his chair and polished off his second drink, rubbing at the back of his neck. "When I found Celeste burned in our bed, I hunted for Ezra. He is lucky I did not find him."

"Ezra ran for years," Killian said, "never settling in one place for long, never leaving a trace of where he'd been."

"It was a different time," Ari added. "Technology has made locating someone far easier."

"Why not kill him now? You have the means and the ability."

Ari's head fell back against the chair, his haunted stare on me. "Seeing what he's done now, I wish I would have. But time heals wounds, and my thirst for vengeance faded when I met your mother. I wanted a quiet life, not another war, so I made peace with my brother."

"Apparently he never made peace with you," I pointed out.

Ari harrumphed. "He has always wanted to rule. He still wants to now, but that wish would only happen if all of my vampires turned against me."

"That would never happen," Killian said with an edge to his voice, "even if a hundred of Ezra's vampires attacked me, your Warden, in their pursuit of Willa."

Ari acknowledged Killian's loyalty with a small smile.

I studied their exchange, pondering everything I heard, but things still didn't add up. "But why is Ezra coming after me? What do I have to do with all this if you've made peace with your brother?"

The grandfather clock chimed two in the morning as Ari's fingers moved restlessly on his empty glass. "When I thought you had died, so did Ezra. But Ezra only seeks one thing."

"Power?" Killian guessed.

Ari nodded and then looked at me. "When your mother and I caged the power, the ripple was felt across the Southwest. Ezra has found that power, and I have it on good authority that he wants to harness it to overthrow me."

Ari rose, moving to the fire, clasping his hands behind his back.

"But it's not something he can simply take. Your mother conjured a lock on the power. Only my blood can access it."

Killian muttered, "Unless someone else from your bloodline could open the lock."

Staring into the fire, Ari nodded.

"That's why he wants me, then?" I asked, hearing the tremble in my voice. "To use my blood to unlock the power?"

"I suspect that is the case," Ari said, turning to face me fully, his neck corded. "He must have discovered the secret Flora was hiding and realized you were still alive. I'm sorry, Willa. I have done this to you."

Everything suddenly hurt, not only my head, but my muscles, stiff and cramping, and I found myself moving toward Ari. "We're going to have this conversation once," I told him, holding on to his arms, "and then we're never going to talk about it again." I pushed past the pain in my throat. "You have suffered as much as I have suffered. You took that power to make the world better, and you've done that. I see your purpose and believe it's a good one. No one could have predicted all that went wrong, and if you could have, you never would have done it. You would have chosen the lives of me and my mother, over making the world better. I have no doubt of that."

I gripped his shoulders tight, staring into his teary eyes.

"We have lost too much time as it is, so please, *please* stop apologizing. I don't blame you. I have nothing to forgive you for. Let's look to the future and make up for all the time we've lost." I hesitated, giving myself a second to change my mind, but my heart knew exactly what I had to say. Not only for Ari, but for me too. "Can you do that for me, *Father*?"

Ari's eyes shined before he wrapped me tightly in his arms. "Yes, my darling Willa, I can do that."

I gave us both the moment we deserved. A long embrace that should have happened a thousand times before now.

When I eventually backed away, I said with a snort, "Besides, I'm pretty sure your asshole brother did this to me. All we need now is a plan to stop him. What do we need to do first?"

"Keep you safe," Killian said, his voice low and smooth. A quick look over my shoulder at him revealed tenderness in his expression. "That is our *only* goal here."

"Great goal, but I also can't hide away forever. Is there no way to destroy the power?"

Shaking his head, Ari said, "At the time, your mother did not know of a spell to destroy the power, only contain it."

"That doesn't mean there isn't one," I said. I looked around the library, taking in the old books that didn't look like fiction. "I assume you have research on this power and on this lock my mother used?"

"I do, yes." With renewed energy, Ari strode to his desk, opening a drawer, revealing a secret drawer underneath. He retrieved a leather-bound notebook. "This is your mother's journal on both the power itself and the magic she used to contain it."

"Thank you," I said, accepting the old notebook and staring at it. I had nothing of my mother's. No personal belongings or gifts ever given by her. I opened the book, the emotion clawing its way up my throat as I touched her hand-writing.

"Will you be all right here for a short time?" Killian asked, brushing his hand over my shoulder. "I'd like to get my team at the Manor searching for Ezra too."

I couldn't even look up as my mother was right here in this journal. I simply waved them off and began to read.

CHAPTER
Eleven

THE POWER ORIGINATED from a magic wielder, who syphoned it from their being and transferred it into a small gemstone the color of a sapphire, but darker and deeper. The stone was ultimately found by a human explorer, who'd heard of Ari's search and brought the information to him for a hefty price. One that Ari had paid without question. Sitting in the wingback chair by the crackling fire, smelling the comforting aroma of the smoky wood, I couldn't help but wonder if Ari thought that price was worth it now that his beloved was gone. He'd done well with the power, made peace between humans and vampires, but the cost was grave.

"You need a break."

I started at Killian's low voice, discovering he'd entered the library at some point and was offering me a teacup on a saucer. "You're right, I probably do need a break." I shut the notebook on my lap and took the tea from him. "Thank you."

He acknowledged my gratitude and then sat opposite me, gesturing at my mother's notebook. "What did you learn?"

"Everything and nothing," I answered with a smile.

One brow lifted. "Care to elaborate?"

I sipped my tea, relishing the honey he'd added. "Everything my mother has written lines up with what Ari has told us so far. My mother was wary of the power." I hesitated, then corrected myself. "Actually, not so much wary as she was aware of the risk of absorbing it."

Of course, Killian read between the lines. "Did she suspect the outcome of what happened to her?"

"I don't think so, but I think she knew there was a possibility that once Ari absorbed the magic, they'd have to expel some of it later."

Imposing and impossibly handsome in his black dress shirt, unbuttoned and rolled at the sleeves, Killian settled back into the chair. "Did she understand the risks of that?"

"From her notes, I'd say yes, but in her writing, I can tell it's a risk she thought they needed to take so that she and Ari, and any other bonded mixed supernaturals, could live together peacefully, along with their offspring."

Tilting his head to the side, Killian's hair fell over his brow. He asked, "Did she note how to destroy the power?"

"Sadly, no. The magic she used to contain this power is called a blood-key spell, which we already know, of course, but without Ari, or a direct descendant's blood, the lock is unbreakable." Even if I had no magic, I was as educated as any witch, having grown up in the Assembly. "From what I read, it's clear my mother's intent was to find a way to destroy the power; she simply needed more time. The plan had always been to keep the power locked away safely until she could end it." I took another sip of the tea before returning the cup to the saucer. "She had some theories on where the power came from. Whatever tests she did on the power revealed it's not white magic from witches, and it wasn't dark magic deriving from vampires either; it was something different, something very old."

"But magic nonetheless?"

"She suspected the magic was elvish, ancient shape-shifters who were brutally hunted during the medieval period. Through her research, she'd uncovered an old scroll that the last remaining elf transferred their magic into the gem to ensure their magic wasn't wiped from the world entirely, in hopes that one day, their bloodlines would be reborn." I paused, recalling what I'd read. "But her notes say that only a powerful magic being could accept the magic without the power killing them, as we saw in Ari. The magic is great, and without the ability to contain all of the power, the energy will destroy the one trying to absorb it."

"Most would die, then?"

"I suspect so, but Ezra is a powerful and old vampire in his own right, and only part of the power is left now." I ran my hands over my tired eyes. A thought so heavy I didn't even want to consider it. When I lowered my hand, I asked, "Has there been any word on Ezra's location?"

"Not yet," Killian reported, leaned forward, resting his elbows on his knees. "We've got scouts out looking for him, as well as anyone within his guard. When they find someone, we will be alerted."

"Good." I sighed.

I took another sip of my tea as Killian asked, with a budding smile, "Just to be clear, we won't solve any more tonight, then?"

The sound of his voice dipping lower made my nerve endings stir and tingle. The hairs on my arms and nape rose at the magic rushing through the space. I sucked in a deep breath, barely able to set my teacup down on the saucer, my hand trembling with the force of the energy flowing over me. "No, we won't solve this tonight," I managed to whisper.

With firm eye contact, he rose and took a step, closing the distance between us.

Then another step.

And another.

Until his hands were braced on the armrest of the chair

and his face closed in on mine. "Then, since we have time, I suggest we get back to those thoughts you had earlier."

Heat sizzled in the air as I ran my hands over his and up his strong forearms. "Haven't forgotten about that, have you?"

"Not for a single moment," he said, his voice rough.

Lost in his eyes, I gingerly caressed the curves of his forearms, his power tingling against my fingers. "Is it always like this?" I asked.

"Like what?" He groaned.

I dragged my touch along the dips of his bicep, his magic burning hotter, tingling faster. "Like *this* with a vampire?" I slowly slid my fingertips up his arm. "I've never been with a vampire before," I admitted. "The intensity when I touch you is like nothing I've ever felt." He shuddered, and I grinned, heat spiraling deep into my core.

He stiffened and his nostrils flared as I flattened my hand, enjoying the flexing of his muscles. "No, it is not." Then his mouth claimed mine, and with that simple touch, he captured my mind, our lips moving in a perfect rhythm.

The library's door slammed shut with the force of Killian's magic, and he murmured against my mouth, "This room is soundproof. No one will get through that door."

I laughed against his lips. "Is that a request for me to be loud?"

"It's a promise that I will make you scream my name, *amare*."

I shivered at the dark lust in his eyes, at his promise. "Is speaking foreign languages part of your foreplay?"

He chuckled, low and deep, and the smooth sound shivered over my flesh as he dropped his head, trailing his nose against my neck. "It can be."

I moaned, angling my head to give him better access, heat and need pulsating between my thighs. "What does that mean, what you called me?"

A pause. Then he looked me dead in the eye. "One night I will tell you."

"But not now?"

"Not now," he murmured, a sinful grin spreading across his face. "Now, I'd rather do something else with our mouths."

His kissing returned to my neck, to my collarbone, to the top of my breast, as each piece of clothing left my body. I eagerly explored him, sliding his shirt up his torso until he removed it swiftly. His pants were gone a moment later, and I allowed myself to take in my fill of him. The fire cast a soft, orangish light across his incredibly toned body, but my gaze fell lower to his impressive cock. Hungry for *that*, I squeezed my thighs together.

I went to move, to *taste* him, to feel that energy he exuded filling my mouth, when Killian groaned, and with a vampiric speed my eyes couldn't register, he had my jeans and panties off, and he went to one knee before the chair. I gripped the armrests breathlessly as he stared at my breasts, my stomach as he stroked me, running his hands over all of me, until his focus narrowed on my sex and he smiled.

"You can taste me," he murmured, pushing my thigh up until it hung over the armrest, "but not before I taste you." When his tongue glided against my drenched heat, I threw my head back and moaned.

Every circle of his tongue had me tightening my fingers on the armrest as he stroked me, until I couldn't take anymore. I ground against his mouth, his power rushing in wild waves over me, taking me higher and higher, the highest I'd ever gone.

Until all that force shattered me, and I came against his mouth with a breathy moan, trembling with my release.

Except my climax didn't calm the desire—it fueled it.

Needing more, and needing it *now*, I reached for his face and sealed my mouth across his, scenting myself on him. I took control of our mouths and thrusting tongues, rising, forcing him to rise with me. I guided him to the chair and kissed his neck, nibbled his ear, ran my tongue down his collarbone, kissed along each shoulder and then moved lower along the dips and curves of his abdomen until I met the pathway of hair leading the way to what I wanted most.

Keeping my eyes on his, I settled onto my knees before him. His hard cock greeted me with a twitch before I took him into my hand and then into my mouth. His low groan made me shiver as I slid my lips up and down him, his magic tingling against my tongue, building as I licked him, taking him deep into my mouth, sucked and played, relishing his urgent moans. His thighs stiffened beneath my hand, and I was suddenly on my feet, straddling him in the chair, his hand around his cock primed at my entrance.

"I need to feel you," was all he said.

I threaded my hands in his hair. "I need you too."

Not waiting, and on magical birth control, I slid down and took him in, painfully slowly to experience every second of the power of Killian filling me completely. My head fell back. I moaned, deeper, louder, as his hands cupped my breasts, massaging, before they explored my body, not missing a single place, only to stop on my buttocks, where he gripped me tight as I rode him.

And he let me, never once taking over, or using his vampire speed to bring me higher, but I wanted him to blow my mind. I wanted to soar. "Harder," I gasped, lowering my gaze to him, finding pleasure parting his lips. "Faster," I begged.

A low growl rumbled from deep in his chest as he gripped one breast, and I shivered at the firm, demanding touch, wanting just that. His other hand gripped my buttock, and then he helped me move … harder … faster … until our moans were blending, and the scent of raw sex filled the air as he brought me higher and higher, my chest brushing against his, skin slapping against skin, our bodies melting into euphoria as he dropped his head into my neck.

I tilted my head offering him access to my jugular.

He dragged his nose along the pulsing vein. Once. Twice. Thrice. "A tempting treat," he finally murmured, lifting his head. The bright silver glow of his eyes burned like hot liquid metal. "But not one I want if you will regret it."

I threaded my hands into his hair, holding him to me. "I won't regret it if you keep your promise to make me scream your name."

His low chuckle had me shivering and shifting my hips, harder, faster, his strength fueling the passion, as his mouth met mine again.

And again.

And again.

Until we were moving fast, sweat coating our bodies, and his mouth left mine, traveling down my neck again.

Yes.

Yes.

Yes.

He placed a gentle kiss along the side of my neck before his fangs pierced my flesh.

I expected pain, but on the contrary, sensation exploded in my core, as Killian suddenly took control of my body, moving me in ways no witch could move. Pounding thrusts sent the chair moving against the hardwood floor until it hit the bookshelf, books falling to the floor. I became silent in the high, against the hold the pleasure had on me. Until Killian sucked deep on my neck, sparks of pleasure burned hotter and hotter and hotter, and only then, as my blood met his lips, did I succumb to the euphoria chasing me. I came undone as Killian bucked and jerked, roaring his release, and I followed him, drowning in the waves of pleasure, and fulfilled his promise: I screamed his name.

———

Hours had gone by, slow, sensual, incredible hours before the lust had quieted to a low hum. Tangled together on the bed in my bedroom after leaving the library, the sheets pushed to the end, sweat slicked my skin, but only my skin, though Killian lay still against the pillow, his eyes shut, hair tousled. I lay tucked into his arm, on my side, his fingertips trailing the curve of my hip. The window was open, the curtains fluttering with the breeze. Ambrose had left the moment he heard a loud whistle outside the window. *Raphael*, Killian had said before his kiss stole my thoughts away and his magic slammed the windows shut. Ambrose hadn't returned, and I got the feeling Killian had requested my dragon stay busy for the night.

The quiet felt good, comfortable, as I ran my touch down the middle of Killian's chest, but my thoughts wouldn't settle. "Did all go well when you returned to the Manor?"

"It did," he confirmed, his voice rough and sleepy. "My guard is ready for anything that awaits us, and Severin is hunting Ezra."

"Is Severin a good friend?"

"He's been my right hand for many, *many* years," Killian said, looking more relaxed than I'd ever seen him. "We fought together in the war, but when I returned to my station after I had been rebirthed to continue to fight in the war, I found him in the hospital with typhoid fever, nearing death."

"So, you offered him immortality?"

A nod. "He was a great man, and he's an even more loyal vampire. I trust him with my life, and more importantly"—he tapped me on the nose—"I trust him with yours."

I smiled, heat radiating through my body. "You two must have had fun together over the years."

He chuckled, sliding his cool fingers along my spine. "A great deal of fun and trouble."

"I can only imagine," I said with a laugh, before I realized that this wasn't only jarring for *me*. "Your vampires must miss you. It must be strange not having you at the Manor."

"It will be good to return home after this."

So, he missed them too. I kissed him on the chin for that, moving on to the next thought spinning in my mind. "Ari said you absorbed more power than the other Wardens. Did you have much power before then?"

His head tilted toward me, revealing sleepy eyes that somehow made Killian look more human. "Some, but I was young when Ari offered me the position of Warden. I had the gift of fire, only in smaller increments. I could burn small objects but was exhausted after."

Killian seemed to live and breathe power, like the magic had always been a part of him. I couldn't imagine him not having his gifts. "If you could go back to that moment when Ari offered you the power, would you still take it?"

He swiped at my hair, sending the strands over my shoulder. "Yes, but not because the power made me stronger. I would have accepted because the Wardens are important to Ari's rule. Without them, peace between humans and vampires would never have happened. The new world Ari dreamed of needs leaders, and I am honored to lead for him."

Hearing Killian's high regard of my father, and knowing of their deep relationship, made me aware of my shortcomings. "Do you feel obligated to protect me?" I asked before I thought better of it.

His fingers froze on their travels over my shoulder. "Obligated in what way?"

"Because I'm Ari's daughter," I said. "He is your Sire, and I just wonder if this … connection—"

He pinched my hip. "What we have has nothing to do with my strong blood bond with Ari."

I leaned up, catching his stern stare. "How can you be sure?"

His touch slid along my back until he cupped my bottom. "Because the connection we have is, feels … *different* than my bond with Ari."

"Well, that's good news," I said, planting a quick kiss on his lips. "You have to admit this connection seems …"

"Intense?" he offered.

I laughed, placing my chin on my hands folded on his chest. "We haven't been able to leave the room, and I can't seem to get enough of you, so yes, intense is a good word."

His eyes searched mine as he tucked my hair behind my ear. "We are lucky to have found each other. I am glad for it."

"Me too." I smiled. "I do have a theory about this connection though."

"What's that?"

"Your bond with Ari, along with having some of his power, may be the reason I was able to talk to you telepathically."

"It is a good theory," he said slowly.

"But you don't believe it?"

He cupped my chin and dragged his thumb across my bottom lip. "I believe anything that comes out of this perfect mouth."

I snorted a laugh. "Now you're just buttering me up."

He barked a laugh, and the sound was so real, so honest, and I knew in that second very few people had ever heard Killian laugh like that, making it even more special. When his laughter faded, his eyes still smiled. "Speaking of you and Ari, things seem to be going well."

"It's an adjustment," I admitted, tracing his strong jawline. "But I'm grateful he's back in my life. Honestly, I'm trying not to overthink all this and just let things be as they want to be. I can't imagine going through what Ari went through. To lose so much, so fast. I think we've all been through a lot, and maybe we all just deserve to have a little bit of happiness in all this hell."

Killian's warm kiss brushed my forehead. "You do deserve that. You both do."

"So do you, you know." When his brows lifted, I smiled. "Happiness, you deserve it too."

He dragged his knuckle across my cheek. "Right now, I am very happy. There is nothing I need. I have a position I enjoy. I am surrounded by friends. And I have you."

"Yes, you do." I smiled.

Curiosity brimmed in his eyes. "We've talked about me, about Anna May and my past, but what about you? Did you have someone who cared for you?"

My heart twisted a little. "I did have someone, for four years."

"A warlock?"

I nodded, sliding my finger along his collarbone. "Mikkel Wildes, son of Eastern High Priestess Esmeralda."

"Ah, I suppose that explains why she was on your side at our meeting. You had a good relationship with her, then?"

"I did. She's a fantastic witch, a good leader. For a time, a motherly figure to me when I lived at the Assembly."

"And Mikkel, what was he like?"

I caught the slight edge to his voice and understood that his opinion of Mikkel would be forged by what I said next. "For four years he was wonderful. We grew up together, learned about life together, had fun together. I thought he was my future."

Killian's fingertips continued traveling over my hip. "Did you walk away or did he?"

"Neither. I failed the rite."

His hand froze. "Are you saying that it was just assumed if you failed the rite, you two would be over?"

I shrugged. "That's the way of the Assembly. I had no power. I would bring nothing to Mikkel's offspring."

"They are fools," Killian growled. "But luckily for me, his

terrible choice means I have you now." He wrapped an arm around my waist, tugging me underneath him, sliding between my thighs. His mouth sealed across mine, and I lost myself in his demanding kiss, a kiss that spoke volumes. That no one would come between us, not Ezra or any other vampire, and certainly not ex-lovers. But he never let the kiss grow hotter. He broke it and turned onto his back, taking me with him. Tucked against his chest again, he asked, "Do you miss your life at the coven?"

"I did, so, so much when I first moved to Charleston," I admitted. "But now, I don't know. Everything's different. I'm different. And I'm not even sure anymore what I missed about living with my coven. Were my friends really my friends if they haven't found a way to contact me?"

Killian pressed his lips against the top of my head, tightening his arms around me. "What I know is nothing would stop you from seeing your friends, and from what I've seen of Gwen and Finnick, nothing would stop them either."

I chuckled, sliding my thigh over his. "We are a force."

"Indeed." He slapped my butt hard, earning a loud squeak, when suddenly his power warmed the room as the windows opened, and Ambrose flew through the opening.

He landed between us and kissed my nose. I kissed him back. "This must be hard for him." I stared into the sweet darkness of Ambrose's eyes, the one solid that had always been in my life. "His whole life has been turned upside down. I really wasn't kidding when I said we had a quiet life. I never went anywhere, did anything, but sit on my rooftop garden and watch him fly."

"Then let's do just that."

I sat up. "What do you mean?"

Killian's gaze went straight to my breasts before moving lower and lower until he met my eyes again with a groan. It looked like it pained him to climb out of bed and step into his pants; his mighty erection had me wondering why he was putting them on. "Let's give him a little bit of normalcy and take him for a fly."

I blinked, then understood his meaning in his dancing eyes. "Wait. Do you mean, flying with him?"

"You've never done so?" Killian asked with a grin.

I leapt up off the bed and hurried into my clothes in a second flat. I'd done many things with Ambrose, but they were all witchy things. This was the very first time I'd do something a dragon would love, beyond feeding him the biggest and best steaks, and for all that had gone wrong lately, I felt lit up inside, running on adrenaline.

As I wiggled into my jeans, I looked to the reason for all the good lately and found Killian already dressed with his vampiric speed, and my insides turned to mush. Because, in the world as I knew it, it was rare to meet anyone who saw me for me and cared about my happiness. Even rarer when they took Ambrose's happiness into account too.

After I finished dressing, I lunged at him, wrapping myself around him. "It feels wrong to say that I'm over-flowing with happiness that you left your mortal life behind so that I could find you now, but I am."

Killian's head dropped to my neck, and as his wintery aroma engulfed me, he pressed a kiss against where he'd bitten me, and I shivered. "It's not wrong when *this* is so right." His arms locked around me, and as I held my breath, his power brushed across my skin as he flew us out the window with Ambrose hot on our heels.

The wind tickled my face as Killian slowed, circling Ambrose, instigating a chase. Then he shot forward hard, and Ambrose flew backward, his eyes narrowing in the hunt, and then charged forward, just as fast. A bubble of happy laughter escaped my mouth as I leaned my head against Killian's chest, the strength of him surrounding me as Killian did one thing with Ambrose no warlock, human, or vampire had ever done: he played with my dragon.

CHAPTER
Twelve

WHEN THE SUN began to rise, heavy thoughts over the blood lock, my friends and Flora had me climbing out of bed. Killian went to check in with Ari's guards, since we hadn't heard if Gwen and Finnick had arrived. While Gwen would have no objection to closing the bookshop, Finnick had obligations to his clients that would take time to resolve. But a deep sleep wouldn't find me until they were safely under Ari's roof.

Standing in the bathroom, I finished applying a coat of mascara after my shower with Killian earlier, my emotions a mix of happiness, satisfaction, fear, and everything in between. Last night, after flying with Ambrose until my dragon grew tired, the lust had only intensified, until I hurt everywhere in the best possible way, bruises along my hips and thighs to prove it. Killian offered more than once to heal me with his blood, but I liked this hurt. The feel of him still on me, inside me, the piney scent of him all over me.

When I came out of the bathroom, dressed for the day, Ambrose suddenly jumped into my arms, fluttering his little wings. "Gotta go out, buddy?" I asked, pressing a kiss to the top of his head.

His wagging tongue was his answer.

I whisked open the door, finding two guards stationed at the ready. They'd been dismissed by Killian last night but were obviously called back when he'd left the room a few minutes ago. I was glad they weren't around last night—I couldn't get enough of Killian. No human or warlock had ever stirred such need in me, but the more time I spent with Killian, the more I wanted him. He had become a drug that I couldn't get enough of—a fix that couldn't be met.

I gave the guards a nod hello, then headed down the hallway before I spotted someone in the garden, sitting in the morning sun. Curious, I hurried my steps as Ambrose led the way down the staircase. I said hello to the staff members I passed. They were cleaning the house and getting everything in order now that the vampires in the Citadel were mostly heading to bed to sleep for the few hours they needed. They needed to rest before their work night began, except for the older vampires in Ari's guard, who were working to hunt down Ezra. The moment I went out the side door to the garden, Ambrose whizzed by me and went straight toward the bushes to relieve himself. I headed for Ari, sitting on a cement bench.

"The sun doesn't bother you at all, huh?" I asked, approaching him.

He turned his head, smiled. "No, the sun hasn't bothered me for some time." He patted the bench next to him. "Come, sit. Enjoy this gorgeous morning with me."

I inhaled the floral scents, sitting next to him, staring out at the garden that one-upped the garden at the Assembly. Every flower I'd ever seen was planted in this space and even some I'd never seen before. "This garden is out-of-this-world gorgeous."

"Your mother planted it."

I glanced sidelong at him; he was watching me. "Did she really?"

Again, he smiled. This time warmer. "You can take a witch out of the Assembly, but you can't take the Assembly out of the witch." I laughed, and he added, "Your mother missed the gardens there, the connection she felt to nature, so we created this together, and every year she added more flowers."

His stooped posture made my heart bleed for him. "This … my returning … it must be very hard on you."

"Seeing you reminds me so much of Zara," he said. "You look so much like her. Your beautiful brown hair"—he tugged at the stands next to my face with his other hand—"the same cheekbones, even the same smile." His eyes crinkled at the corners. "To know I still have you is a gift I never expected."

I glanced out at the peonies. "I remember that smell."

"Peonies were your mother's favorite flower."

"Were they really?" He gave a slow nod, and I added, "I have no memories of her. I've seen a few photographs though."

Ari's lips thinned. "Flora never spoke of Zara to you?"

"No, never." At his flat look, narrowed eyes, I hastened to explain, "I only asked about my mother a few times, and I saw the pain it caused Flora. When I was older, and she explained how painful my mother's death was for her, I never asked again."

Ari frowned, staring coldly at the flower bed in front of him. "I could say a million wonderful things about your mother, but I can also show you my memories of her, if you would like that." He held out his hand.

Could I handle this? Could I *see* my mother's love, without ever truly experiencing it?

"Yes, I would love to see her and what our life was like, if that's okay."

"Of course, my darling," said Ari tenderly.

I placed my hand in his, and as his magic rushed over me in a dark wave that should have felt all wrong, and yet didn't, I gasped, falling deep into the past. Ari's memories flashed through my mind, little moments that meant the world to him. With every flash of light, I witnessed every happy moment Ari had ever experienced with Zara from the time they met, to their bonding ceremony, to my birth, and every birthday afterward. All the little things that made up their wonderful life together.

I didn't even realize I was crying until Ari brushed a tear from my cheek after the memories faded, and my mind belonged to me once again. "Ah, Willa, your mother would not want you to cry for her. Zara was full of life and joy, and she would want *that* to be remembered, not all that was lost."

Feeling happy to have ever experienced such love and devastated I couldn't remember any of her, I wiped away the tear trailing down my face. "She was … *incredible*." Zara was all the things I would have wanted. Her smile whenever Ari or I was nearby. Her laughter at all the funny moments life threw her way. Her beautiful singing to me while she rocked me as a baby, to her chasing me around a tree being the scary monster I was running from as a toddler. "I wish I … I wish I had more time with her."

"I wish that too," Ari said. "She was a stunning witch. A witch who had me fighting to change our worlds just so I could have her. There was no one before her and no one after, only her."

"Is that why you sit out here, to remember her?"

Ari stared at the flowers, his gaze so far away. "Every morning when the sun rises, I see her here. In the peonies. In my memories. I remember all the reasons she fought for what we did."

I squeezed his hand. "Was it worth it, even knowing now that, to accept the power would have cost her her life, would you still have made the same decision?"

Ari cupped my cheek. "My only regret is her life was lost and not mine. But I will not break my vow to her. I will see what we hoped for, a world without division, where witches and vampires and humans can live harmoniously." Again, he stroked my cheek. "Where you are accepted without question."

"That is a beautiful dream," I agreed, wrapping my arms around him, leaning my head on his shoulder.

He kissed the top of my head. "It is."

A long, quiet moment passed as Ambrose flew around the garden.

We stayed that way for a while, until he reached into his pocket and pulled out a pear-shaped opal necklace. "I gave this to your mother the night we completed the bonding ceremony. She hadn't been wearing it when she died, worried that if she did, the magic would transfer to the stone." He held the necklace out to me.

I opened my hand and he dropped it in my palm, weighted with power. "It's stunning."

"It is, though it was far lovelier on Zara." He held out his hand, so I set the necklace back into his palm. He rose, moving in behind me and clasping the necklace around my neck. "Your mother would have wanted you to have this to keep you safe, always protected." He smiled. "Ah, it's as stunning on you as it was on her."

"Thank you," I said, touching the smooth, warm opal. An opal stone absorbs the energies of those near it, including negative and harmful ones, and casts them back to their source.

With a long sigh, a very unexpected human move from an old vampire, Ari said, "I'm aware all of this is unsettling and that I'm a stranger to you, but I'd like for us to get to know each other, and I'd like you to be a part of my life."

"I saw the memories," I said. "I saw the love for me in your eyes. I saw the love we had as a family. Yes, you are a stranger to me, but you weren't always. You were my father, and I want you to be again."

"Nothing would bring me more joy." His voice shook as

he pulled me into a hug—the longest hug I'd ever had in my life. I didn't want to let go; Ari's arms felt safe ... like ... *home.*

"I'm sorry to interrupt," Killian said, standing several feet from us, looking down at the paving-stone pathway.

I pulled back. "What's wrong?" I asked with a sinking feeling in my gut.

"Gwen and Finnick are missing."

———

Ari stormed back into the house, barking orders on his way down to the command center, leaving me behind, feeling weightless, like I couldn't get enough air into my lungs. Killian silently followed me, his resounding strength at my back, as I went to the sitting room, a sour taste at the back of my throat. I paced in front of the stone fireplace, nibbling on my thumb. The fire suddenly blazed, and I assumed Killian had done that to comfort me.

My friends were gone ... and I was the reason.

I nearly sank to my knees when Killian wrapped his arms around me from behind. "This is not your fault."

I turned to look up into his eyes even though my shame made me want to hide. "We were lost in each other, enjoying ourselves when my best friends were taken."

Killian locked me into his hold, but he couldn't chase away the chill. "We had no idea what was going on, and your first reaction once you did know was to bring your friends here."

My stomach roiled. "What if Ezra hurts them?"

"He won't," Killian said, adamant.

"How can you be so certain?"

The fire crackled as he released one arm to stroke my cheek. "Because he'll need them as bargaining chips."

"Oh Goddess." The room suddenly becoming impossibly hot. I gripped Killian's shirt. "We have to get them back.

Right now, Killian. We need to find them and help them." My voice broke. "I need them here, with me. I can't lose them."

"You won't," Ari announced tightly, entering the room with Darick hot on his heels.

Darick dropped to one knee before me, bowing his head. "I'm sorry, Princess. Please forgive me."

The silence felt heavy as I absorbed that title, one I certainly did not want. I stepped out of Killian's hold and pulled Darick up by his arms. "First, please do not call me that ever, *ever* again. Second, you have nothing to feel sorry about. This isn't your fault."

"I was tasked with finding them," Darick stated, pulling at the sleeve of his suit. "And I failed you."

All of our guilt wouldn't find Gwen and Finnick. "You need to snap out of this. If you do anything for me, do that. I need you sharp and ready. No more guilt, all right?"

A breeze fluttered the hair around my face as he rose in vampiric speed, and at normal speed, he gave a strong nod. "Yes, ma'am."

"Good," I said, desperate to get my feet back on solid ground. "What have you got so far? Is it Ezra who has them?"

Darick headed to the antique writing desk against the wall closest to the arched doorway. "We don't know."

I blinked. "If you don't know, then how do you know they were taken?"

Darrick sat down, opening his laptop. "Gwen was last seen leaving the bookshop." A few clicks of his fingers, and soon, video surveillance across the street from my bookshop appeared on the monitor, showing Gwen locking up the door. She waved to someone passing by and then walked in the opposite direction. The moment she vanished from view, Darick clicked the pause button. "She was taken somewhere between your bookshop and the next store." Another click of his finger displayed the front door of the dog groomer, who was my neighbor. "Gwen never makes it to this door."

"That's like three steps away," I said to myself more than to anyone else.

"I know, it's odd," Darick agreed. A few more hits of his fingers, and Finnick was seen leaving his real estate office and never makes it to the coffee shop next door. "Your friend Finnick was taken in a similar manner."

"Who could have teleported them?" I whispered, never feeling quite as helpless as I did right now. I looked to Killian to Ari.

Killian frowned at the monitor, his arms crossed. "If they were teleported, I would think there would be a struggle before they were whisked away."

"Very few teleporters work that fast," Ari agreed, scratching the back of his neck, leaning closer to the monitor. "I only know two. One is in my guard. The other is in Killian's."

When Finnick teleported, it took him a handful of seconds to blink out of existence. My throat was closing up as the sitting room began to shrink around me. Killian uncrossed his arms, and I walked straight into his vibrating power. "What can we do to find them?"

Darick responded, "We've got some vampires on the ground, searching for any trace they can follow."

I sighed. "We could really use the witches' help right now." Witches could follow magical imprints left by a vampire.

From his spot behind Darick's chair, Ari tilted his head toward me. "Now you understand what your mother and I were trying to do. The benefit of working together would help all supernaturals."

I knew for a fact, the Assembly wouldn't help us, wouldn't help me. *Think, Willa.* These were my friends; this was my life. I was so damn sick of feeling out of control.

Darick hit a few more buttons on his keyboard and Finnick faded from the monitor. Another few clicks later, the inside of my bookshop appeared on the screen. "Report," Darick said.

"No one is here," the vampire responded through static.

The video jumped and shook, and it occurred to me then, we were watching through Ari's guard's body camera. He was walking through my bookshop, scanning the area, revealing three other vampires with him, all wearing black cargo pants and black shirts.

Ari asked, "Do you see any traces, feel any lingering power?"

A pause. "There is nothing, King. No power. Nothing."

Killian growled. "How can that be?"

I tried to move, tried to speak, tried to do ... *anything* ... but I could only gulp down breaths, falling to my knees. Ambrose came to me, whimpering. I couldn't see him through my blurred vision, my heartbeat thumping in my ears. I vaguely heard Ari and Killian talking before Ari gave Darick orders, but I couldn't make out sounds, only the roaring in my head.

A soft touch grazed my hand. *Ambrose.* And then a finger tucked under my chin, forcing me to look up. *Killian.* He was down on one knee before me.

"We will find them," he promised.

I grasped his forearms, the strength there, hoping to ground myself. "Why is this happening? I didn't want any of this. I wanted a quiet life, with my friends and my bookshop."

Muscles strained beneath Killian's skin. "You will have answers, Willa, and we *will* locate your friends."

"How?" I managed to choke out. "They're just ... *gone.*"

The hesitation before Killian spoke declared that the challenge ahead was not an easy one, but his voice did not waver as he said, "Ezra will have only taken them to get closer to you. That is where he's gone wrong, because, just for thinking he can get close to you, I will bleed him dry." His thumb brushed my cheek, and I leaned into his touch, letting the warmth of his magic comfort me. "I'm afraid this is where we must part ways for the time being. I cannot find your friends from here, but it's not safe for you to leave. Ari will remain at the Citadel with you."

"I'll stay," I told him. "Of course, I'll stay. I'm safe here." A magic-less witch, a vampire without powers … I was a liability.

He plucked my thoughts right out of my head. "You're not a liability, you're a treasure that needs to stay protected. You cannot lose your friends. I cannot lose you."

The statement was so bold that it took my breath away. But the truth in his eyes made me believe him. My head was spinning all over again when I cupped his face. "I cannot lose you either. You need to come back, safe, whole."

He arched one eyebrow. "You think Ezra can hurt me?"

"You are powerful," I said, my fingers twitching to keep him there. "But so is Ezra."

"Ah, but I have something that Ezra does not." His power caressed my cheeks as he cupped my face, smirking. "You, waiting for me. I will come back to you. I will put an end to this."

"Yes, come back to me," I whispered, even though everyone could hear it. I didn't care who was there; I grabbed his shirt and pulled him into me, my mouth meeting his.

Voices suddenly filled the room as Ari's guards moved into the space, all discussing plans of attack, and we broke off the kiss.

Killian stayed on one knee before me, staring into my eyes like we were the only ones in the room.

He held my gaze as I stood with him, and then nodded before following the others out, taking all the air from my lungs with him.

CHAPTER
Thirteen

IN THE HOURS that passed since Killian walked out the door, Raphael had come to take Ambrose to eat and for a fly, and Ari had gone to speak to the other Wardens to prepare their guards for a battle against Ezra. To keep my mind occupied, I spent the remainder of my time reading my mother's journal, not finding anything more than I had already learned. Her studies were unfinished. I retreated to the garden.

I walked along the stone paths, moving through the flowers. This seemed so unreal. For years, I struggled to fit in, to find my place in the world, and now that I had, I was being threatened. Finding out I was part vampire should have been the greatest day of my life. I had a family, a father, best friends who loved me, and a vampire who was making every other lover before him seem inadequate. But vampires were tearing apart everything I cared about. I fingered the necklace around my neck, praying to the Goddess. And I walked the paths.

Again.

And again.

And again.

"Please, Willa, can I get you anything?"

I stopped when I reached the bench and glanced back. Raphael wrung his hands together, bouncing from foot to foot. Poor vampire was a *helper*. Every ten minutes, he'd come by wanting to bring me food, run me a bath. The only thing I needed was Gwen and Finnick here in this house, and for Killian to come home safe. Nothing else mattered, but I began to feel bad I wasn't letting him help. "I could go for a hot chocolate, if you've got that."

His eyes brightened as he rocked back on his heels. "With marshmallows?"

"Yes, that sounds wonderful. Thank you, Raphael."

With vampire speed, he vanished, the door to the house shutting behind him, when a surge of power brushed across my flesh.

"Willa."

The familiar voice had me whirling around with a gasp. I blinked twice, wondering if my eyes were betraying me.

My aunt was standing near the peonies. Flora's bright blue eyes were guarded, her long brown hair pulled back in her usual tight bun. She wore a long black skirt with a dark green blouse and black shawl over her shoulders. "Flora," I gasped, my hand flying to my chest.

"Come, my child," she said, offering her hand with her red-painted fingernails. "We don't have long. I know you have questions. Let me answer them."

I stared at her hand, and for an unknown reason, I hesitated, taking a step back.

Her eyes widened, and in the next breath, her magic lashed out over the garden, creating a bubble around us. "We only have a few minutes to talk before my magic fails and the vampires are alerted to my presence." She took another step toward me, latching on to my hands before I could move away. "You are not safe here. We must leave."

"Ari is my father," I blurted out.

"Yes, but there are reasons I kept that knowledge from

you," Flora said quickly. "You cannot trust him. You cannot trust any of them."

I stared into the eyes of the woman I knew so well, the woman I loved. The very witch that tucked me into bed every night as a child, sang me lullabies, read me stories to chase away bad dreams. "I don't understand any of this," I said, tearing my hands away, taking another step back. "You left the Assembly. You kept the truth about my past from me. How can I trust you now?"

"Because your mother trusted me to raise you," she said urgently, her gaze darting over the garden. "She asked me if she were to ever die that I take you, protect you from him."

"From Ari?"

Flora closed the distance again, her voice shaking. "Yes, Willa, listen to me. Your mother told me about Ari's thirst for power. She also told me when the power became too much. That *his* thirst for power became too much. It terrified her."

"But that doesn't make sense. He wanted to get rid of the power."

She dropped her hands on my shoulders, leaning into my face. "Only because the magic was going to kill him. If it had not been the case, he would have kept the full force of that power. All of it, Willa. Do you not understand who Ari truly is? He's a vampire who wants to rule, not lead among other vampires—*rule.* Why do you think his brother is so determined to stop him?" She cupped my face, her eyes pleading, a bead of sweat appearing at her hairline. "You cannot trust what he tells you. Now, because of him, you are drawn into this war between Ari and Ezra, and you will be killed for it, all because you have Ari's blood." Her hands tightened around my face, her voice cracking with emotion. "You must come with me. Now. Your mother did not want this life for you. She wanted better for you."

I tried to take all this in but failed miserably. "I read her journal. She wanted to help Ari. I saw his memories of her. She adored him."

"No, that is where you're wrong. She only wanted to help you. Your mother wanted you to live a life filled with love, with a father and a mother." She glanced at the magic shimmering around us, frowning as the power seemed to be wavering. "We need to get you to safety. Please, my child, come with me."

I wanted answers so badly I could taste it, and when it came right down to it, while Flora had to banish me by the laws of the Assembly, she did love me. "Okay, I'll give you time to explain."

She stroked my cheek. "Good, my sweet Willa."

A flash of light burst across my vision, and I squeezed my eyes tight as the wind roared around me, until the blinding light faded. When I opened my eyes, a dark forest lay spread out around me. Mature trees hugged a stone pathway long ago abandoned, long, thick vines overgrowing on the stones.

"Come, this way," said Flora, sliding her arm through mine. "Now ask me your questions."

I matched her stride, the forest quiet around us, not even a cricket within earshot. "Ari had thought I died, which meant you were there when my mother performed the blood-lock spell."

"I was."

I glanced sidelong, gauging her reaction. "Did they know you were there?"

She stared straight ahead, taking long strides. "No, I conjured a spell to stay hidden, but I was so worried about Zara, I had to be there." A branch cracked under Flora's foot, the only break in the heavy silence. "And my instincts were right, the spell failed, and you would have been killed had I not swiftly taken you away."

At her steady, lower-pitched voice, I stopped walking,

truly looked at her. "You honestly believed Ari was such a risk to me that you abducted me from my own father?"

"Yes," Flora said, giving a curt nod. "Ari is a power-hungry fool. His thirst for power killed Zara. Of course I kept him from you. He'd only kill you too."

"Because he has enemies?"

Flora pressed her lips together before she tugged on my arm again, walking us forward once more along the over-grown pathway. "Ari cannot love, not truly; he only takes. And he took the greatest thing from both of us—your mother."

Something wasn't adding up. Ari's memories had showed me a happy life, a loving bond between him and my mother. Memories couldn't be falsified. A deep throb began pounding in my temple. I rubbed at the pain and asked, "Why did you leave the Assembly? The high priestesses are looking for you."

She tapped my arm resting on hers. "Because they would not understand that I needed to find you by any means necessary. You know how it is, Willa; they banished you for not coming into your magic. They never would have helped me."

"If you'd told Esmeralda the truth, she might have."

Flora's nose wrinkled. "Esmeralda has dreamy ideals that will never make witches stronger."

Her laughter made me fall back, pulling my arm from hers. She'd laughed like that when the Assembly disagreed with her desire to not accept the treaty of peace made with Ari. At the time, I did not understand her motives, or why it infuriated her so much that the witches were agreeing to peace. Now, however …

"Why am I here, Flora?" I glanced around the dark forest, finally realizing the silence was a whisper of danger.

Pushing up her sleeves, my aunt strode forward, her skirt trailing behind her over the rocky ground. "Because you will change everything, Willa."

Not to save you. Not because I love you. *Because you will change everything, Willa.*

My blood chilled as I took a step. Then another. And another.

I followed her into a clearing where a massive oak tree stood in the center, its branches low to the ground, sprawling over the forest floor. Power drew me forward, rich, pulsating energy that felt oddly familiar, and suddenly I realized exactly where my aunt had brought me.

"I care for you, Willa," my aunt said behind me. "But sacrifices must be made. Your mother was not strong enough to make them. She let her heart lead her. I will not be bound by my emotions."

Immense crackling magic drew me closer to the oak tree. My bloodline was bound to this great elvish magic, and I could sense that connection calling to me with every step. Even as I reached out my hand, stroking the branch, my fingers vibrated with the power flowing through the tree.

Yours.

Yours.

Yours.

The power called to me, a rhythmic plea. Until screaming sent birds fluttering from the trees, and I whirled on the breeze, discovering two bodies bound to another tree by magical bindings, bowing and twisting in agony at the magical lashes burning their flesh.

Gwen … Finnick …

CHAPTER
Fourteen

"WHAT HAVE YOU DONE?" I breathed to Flora. My best friends sagged against the magical bindings, out cold, before their vampiric healing awakened them again, and they opened their eyes, their anguished gazes locked on to me. I was rooted to the spot, wrapping my arms around my middle, my thoughts fuzzy. The fact that Finnick wasn't tele-porting them away and Gwen remained in her vampire form indicated the magical bindings hindered their abilities.

"This was never my plan," said Flora, moving close to the oak tree. "When your mother perished, I took you, protected you, shielded you from the danger that your mother put you in."

"She never asked you to look after me, did she?" I said slowly. "You stole me from my father."

Flora reached the tree, her expression pinched as she dragged her hand along the branch of the tree. "You mother had been corrupted by *him*. Turned to believe that being with a vampire was right, but the sin was great, and she paid for it with her life." Minutely shaking her head, she tapped her fingers against the old wood. "You were just a wee babe at the time. I refused to allow her wrongs to destroy your life too."

Her chin lifted, and she stopped next to Gwen and Finnick. "To fix her wrongs, I raised you right, waited for you to come into your power. I planned to tell you about your father then, but you never came into your magic." She was like a stranger to me, this bitter witch. "You were supposed to be the strongest of us. With Zara's power, along with Ari's, you should have been able to lead witches into the future, where we stand above the vampires. Where *we* lead. But the sin of your mother extended to you, and the Goddess refused to accept you as a witch, with that tainted blood running through your veins."

The words hit home. And hit hard.

I struggled against the magic to take a step back. "Why are you doing this?" Even I heard the tremor in my voice.

Her intense, fevered eyes shifted. "I'm doing this to right a wrong. Witches are not strong enough to defeat Ari. But with this power, *I* can be. Whoever gets the gifts left by the elves will lead, Willa."

Breathless, I managed to say, "All of this, from the very beginning, has been about you?"

She sighed exaggeratedly. "No, Ezra is hunting you for this power, my dear, but his actions forged my decision to break the lock. We cannot let another vampire take this power. It will only lead to darkness."

Even with Gwen and Finnick shaking uncontrollably, limp against the tree, at my aunt's feet, to believe she could do this was impossible. "Flora, how can you—"

"How can I *what*?" she said, her tone scathing. "Want for a better world for witches? Not allow another vampire to take power he shouldn't have. Elvish magic is good and white and clean. This power belongs to a witch."

A wave of magic thickened the air, and Gwen and Finnick bowed, shrieking as Flora whipped out a band of bright white magic, cutting into their flesh, ripping at their clothes.

"Stop," I cried, running to them. I sank to my knees,

digging at the earth when I couldn't get past the magic bubble surrounding them. "Stop hurting them. Please, Goddess, just stop."

"All you need to do, Willa, is unlock the power," said Flora from somewhere behind me. "Break the lock, and I will absorb the elvish magic. After that, I give you my word that you can walk away with your friends. You can return to Charleston and live your life there."

My chest heaved as I glanced back over my shoulder at her. "I can't trust you now. Let them go and I'll help you."

Flora's mouth curled. "There will be no bargaining here. One day you will understand why I had to go to such measures."

"I will *never* forgive you for this," I said through gritted teeth. "How could you do this to my mother? You were her sister; she loved you. How could you do this to me?"

Skin stretching into a snarl, Flora said, "Your mother failed you. If you are to blame anyone, blame her. She never should have allowed Ari to have this power, and now I am tasked to fix her mistakes." A tendril of her magic shivered across me until a dagger appeared in front of me. "Cut yourself. Your blood on the roots will open the lock, and you and your friends can walk away."

I had to stop her.

Screaming cut through the forest. Lash against lash of magic rained down on Gwen and Finnick, their cries echoing against the night sky, as their clothes were ripped away, revealing deep gashes along their backs, arms, stomach.

Blood coated their bodies. Their mouths were open wide as they screamed. "No more," I begged, reaching for the dagger. "I'll break the lock."

I wrapped my hand around the metal dagger. I lifted the blade to my arm, when a low voice I'd heard a thousand times over the radio said, "Yes, you will break the lock."

Gasping, I dropped the dagger as I saw vampires arrive in

the clearing. I crawled back, hitting the tree trunk, but the pain never registered, as one by one, hundreds of vampires blinked into existence.

One vampire stood out among them. *Ezra.*

Holding his hands loosely behind his back, he surveyed the scene with a steely gaze, his blue eyes the same shade as mine, as Ari's. He wore navy dress pants and a lighter blue button-up, his dark hair styled. Slightly shorter and thinner than my father, Ezra was no less imposing.

"Flora," said Ezra. "This is an unexpected surprise."

My aunt moved closer to me, to guard her prize. The notes in my mother's journal indicated that when the power was released, it clung to the first magic user it could find, whether that person was deserving of it or not. Something I suspect that elf who bound its magic into the gem would have regretted if they had known this would be the outcome.

"Ezra," my aunt sneered, a vein throbbing in her neck.

The magical bindings on Gwen and Finnick suddenly disappeared as Flora pulled back her magic to defend herself against Ezra and his legion of vampires. I mouthed, *"Go."*

They clung to each other. Tears flooded their faces as they adamantly shook their heads.

"We're not leaving you," Gwen mouthed.

Tears sprang to my eyes, manic energy shaking my limbs: *"Please. Go."*

"No," Finnick wordlessly cried.

Ezra and Flora continued to taunt each other, their voices filling the silence in the forest, but I stared upon my friends, the two vampires who welcomed me in, although I was different. Two friends who loved me deeply when no one else did. Heart racing, I gripped the damp grass below me. *"You need to live,"* I implored. *"You won't if you stay here. Please, if you love me, you'll do as I ask and go."*

Finnick's eyes stared sightlessly, and I sighed in relief that my friends would not die here tonight.

"No—" Gwen screamed out loud.

Then they were gone, only crumbled leaves where they'd once been.

I shut my eyes, Ezra and Flora's continued taunts in my ears, but I felt detached.

Alone.

Again, I was alone.

And I would die alone.

Killian, I need you …

In the darkest moment of pain, it occurred to me my life was repeating itself, and I was stuck in a loop I never asked for and that I couldn't break free from.

Alone.

Alone.

Alone.

Ezra's growl made even the trees sway. "Walk away or die, Flora; that is my offer to you in respect for the Assembly. My qualm is not with the high priestesses, and it is not my choice to end you tonight."

I reopened my eyes, feeling like I existed outside my body, watching my aunt—or the stranger she'd become—staring down Ezra like she had a fighting chance against him and his vampires.

"This power is akin to a witch's power." Flora squared her shoulders, showing the palms of her hands, the roar of her magic causing the hairs on my arms to rise. "It does not belong to a vampire. You will not have it."

"I will be different from my brother," Ezra purred, a gleam in his eye. "I will be better."

Magic pulsed above, below, and around me, as Flora raised her hands, and then white light blasted across the dark sky toward Ezra and his vampires. And yet no one moved. The energy hit a shield around the group, and like a sponge to water, the shield absorbed the magic in a swift sizzle. Flora's eyes bulged, the unknown in their depths, revealing all the questions in my mind of how Ezra was conjuring such a shield.

I never got an answer, and neither did Flora.

A *crack* followed by a breeze blew my hair around my face. Then any remaining heat leached from my bones as a *thud* echoed across the forest, and Flora's decapitated head rolled toward me.

CHAPTER
Fifteen

I TRIED DESPERATELY to look away from the emptiness in my aunt's eyes, the death there, the finality, but I froze in the chill washing over me. The world seemed to go still around me, the silence now a loud hum pounding in my ears.

"Niece." Ezra's dress shoes stepped on Flora's hair.

My stomach roiled and I held back a scream, meeting Ezra's cold, calculating eyes. I had no words, no breath, no *anything* to help me. My aunt was *gone*. I hated her for what she'd done, for the danger she put me in, but she was … *gone*.

Ezra squatted in front of me, taking my chin in his grip. "Do not be as foolish as your aunt," he said, his voice soothing. "Do not fight me."

"I don't want any of this," I managed to choke out, staring at him without seeing him clearly. "I never wanted any of this."

"Be that as it may, your blood is all I need to open the lock and end this once and for all."

His finger dragged against my cheek, and I jerked away. "Don't touch me." I growled an animalistic sound I'd never heard escape my mouth before.

Chuckling, he finally removed his hand from my face, a

single onyx band around his ring finger. "You look very much like your mother, a beautiful witch she was. It is a shame what happened to Zara. My quarrel was never with her."

My breaths were loud, my chest heaving. "Never speak of my mother."

"Oh, you misread me," Ezra said before cackling. "I have the utmost respect for your mother. Without her, the elvish magic would have never been found, so for that, I will forever be grateful to her. But to not share the power was selfish, not only of her, but of Ari, something I told my brother more than once." With a huff, he rose, towering over me. "It is both a shame and a blessing that you are from my brother's blood-line. I need you now to break this lock, but I regretfully cannot let you live after you do, as you will always be a threat to me."

I parted my lips to say *something*, to give myself more time, but his cold stare kept the words from escaping my mouth.

Death hungered for a soul tonight.

Over the years, I'd heard stories that when a witch was facing death she saw flashbacks of her life, moments of all the happiest times, but I only saw an icy, brutal end that I couldn't stop. Every second felt slower than the last as Ezra took another dagger from the sheath at his waist. But as I dug my fingers into the warm earth, I hit the steel of the blade Flora had placed in front of me. I inched my fingers toward the hilt as Ezra leaned in, and when he grabbed for my hand, I lurched up, stabbing forward.

He roared as I sliced his forearm, blood flowing from the wound on the leafy floor.

"Stay away from me," I snarled, holding the dagger out.

Ezra chuckled, as did the vampires at his back. "You are surrounded by my vampires, niece. Do you truly think you'll escape?"

"Probably not," I spat, baring my teeth. "But if I'm going down bleeding, so are you."

The low laughter echoing across the forest caused the hairs to raise on the back of my neck.

Until that callous, ruthless laughter died, and a pair of glowing silver eyes shone in the darkness. Warmth slid across me, comfortable and loving, as a familiar power brushed against my senses. The dagger shook in my hand at the scent of snowy pine, and my heart leapt in joy.

Killian.

A roar shook the trees as Ezra suddenly went soaring back. Killian had shoved him away. The unexpected release of all my tension left my entire body shaking—as Killian took position in front of me, his stance wide, at the ready. Next to him, Severin stood, dagger drawn.

"Brother," Ari said, cool and collected, stepping out the shadows, his guards following, circling around him. "I have been looking for you."

Ezra pushed himself up from the ground in a blink of an eye, spittle flying from his mouth as he cried, "You will not stop me this time, Ari. The power shall be *mine*." With a battle cry, he lunged at Ari, and his vampires followed him.

Vampires became a blur around me, bodies dropping, heads rolling, flesh burning as I pressed myself against the tree, feeling almost as if it were wrapping its branches around me to offer protection.

The branches soon swayed with force as Ari's blast of power rushed over the forest, but Ezra did not fall, the shield around him protecting him from Ari's magic. I scanned the area. Killian had not fallen.

Power brushed across my skin, as I tilted my head to the side, leaning into this titillating energy. I turned inward toward the sweet warmth reaching out to me from the branches of the trees. I searched through the powers there. Two were familiar to me, but neither was pulsating, asking me to take hold of the magic. I circled myself around the strongest power, the one roaring, sizzling through my veins, and as the power reached out, caressing at my blood, I'd met the source with tenderness in my heart.

It answered back with a gentle stroke, and somehow, I knew exactly what I needed to do.

"Killian," I called into the battle.

Glowing eyes met mine as he halted, vampires grabbing at him. "It will never end if I don't stop it."

I'd been there when this lock was forged, and only *I* could set all this right, absorbing a power that would ultimately kill me, as magic-less as I was. I would destroy the elvish power forever with my death. "I'm sorry we didn't get more time."

Ari stepped out of the battle and reached for me, his energy causing the vampires lunging at him to explode.

Killian roared against the vampires grabbing at him, his power cracking like lightning in the still air. "Willa ..."

I did not hesitate. I touched the oak tree's root, tingling with the power, took hold of it, and grabbed Flora's blade on the ground. I sliced deep into my forearm, my blood spilling on the roots.

"Stop her," Ezra shrieked.

But he was too late.

A loud *bang* shook the forest floor, the power pulsating as the lock broke free. Light poured out of the tree, the magic reaching out to me. With an open mind and heart, I claimed the gift.

The energy began seeping into the air. I sensed the tendrils reaching out, and I stroked them back, like a friend offering a hug. But within the power, I discovered four different sources twined together in these roots. Each carried its own strength and weight, but only one energy in the roots felt personal.

As I reached out to touch that power, it felt like coming home, to the home I had never known. I called to the power: *I am yours*. Again and again, I whispered the words. The power wove its way through my blood until all my broken pieces felt wholly remade.

Then another, different power confronted me.

I sank into its pureness, its rawness. I was unafraid. Not afraid to die. To accept what I faced in the afterlife. I dropped my guard and welcomed that power inside.

It hit me like a train at full speed as light stormed through my body, and for a moment, I was no longer on the ground. I floated within the power as the elvish magic met mine.

A laugh passed my lips at the joy of feeling so strong, so … *whole*.

I opened my eyes.

Bodies scattered the forest, the grass dripping with blood and death. Before, the fighting had been a blur around me, but now I could see everyone clearly as if time had slowed. Ezra and Ari were fighting, daggers drawn, cuts and lashes covering their bodies, but Ari's magic couldn't touch Ezra through the shield protecting him. Killian was fighting his way toward me, his neck corded, his forearms, ridged and defined. I inhaled sharply, scents overwhelming me, a hunger raging. But only one aroma caught my attention. A smell of pine and snow, with the sweetest undercurrent now running beneath it, a scent so delectable, I refused to wait to taste it.

Consumed by it, desperate to have a simple lick of such pleasure, I pulled deep on what I wanted. To be alone with that scent. With only that need in my mind, I drew on the power tingling along my skin and told it only one thing: *protect the ones I love and the ones they love*.

And with a lash of blue light, the power answered.

CHAPTER
Sixteen

"WILLA." Killian's breathy whisper drew me back to him, pulled me out of the warmth, out of the rich power. Our enemies were dead on the ground. But I found *him.*

"Talk to me," Killian said. Tell me you're all right."

I parted my mouth to explain that the blood-lock spell my mother created had somehow stripped my magic away and contained it, and now that I had my witch powers, which felt vast and endless, I *also* had the strength to absorb the elvish magic as mine. And a swipe of my tongue along one fang, and then another confirmed that my witch roots weren't the only roots I got back.

Killian's eyes widened, and he dragged his thumb across one of my fangs.

A thirst I'd never known overtook me, and I lunged at Killian, his devilish smile at my vampiric speed his only reaction before I straddled his lap, dragging my nose against his skin. Goddess, his scent was like no other, a smell making me both desperate and painfully thirsty.

One of his arms came around my back, holding me tight to him. The other threaded into my hair. "Drink, *amare,*" he murmured.

Need had me sinking my fangs deep into his neck. His deep groan stormed across me with sizzling heat, and I sucked deeper, moaning with every long pull I took from his neck. Everything was louder around me, the *swish* of the branches moving on the breeze, the rustle of fabric on bodies as he held me close, intimately, while I took my fill of him.

More …

"Zara."

I licked the blood on my lips, momentarily trapped by Killian's eyes before I looked behind him. To Ari. I lurched to my feet, with Killian joining me, his hand gripping mine tight.

I'd seen the photographs of Zara. Ari's memories too. But now she stood next to the tree in the flesh. A gorgeous, dark-haired witch, with soft and trusting green eyes, and it occurred to me that Ezra wasn't wrong. Except for the different eye color, I looked very much like my mother.

Tears ran down her face as she whispered, "Ari."

In a rush, he gathered her in his arms and kissed her, their sobs carrying in the night sky. "How can this be?" he cried. "My Zara, how can you be here?"

"I am home," she said, weeping, gripping his bloody and ripped shirt. "That's all that matters, Ari. I am home now."

Long moments passed as they held each other, until my mother finally stepped away, her gaze meeting mine. Slowly, she took a step toward me.

Then another.

Until she stood in front of me.

Zara was everything I'd expected, stunning, a little taller than me with the same shade of hair as mine. But her expression was so full of the motherly love I missed in my life that tears I could not stop rose in my eyes.

She cupped my face. "Can it be? Is this grown woman my Willa?"

"Mom," I managed to choke out.

"Yes, my darling." She kissed one of my cheeks then the other. "I am home," she repeated as if even she couldn't believe it. Her arms came around me like a lock that could never be broken, and I melted into her hold. She held me in a way I had never been held before, so familiar and comforting, *a mother's hold*. I did not count the minutes she held me as we cried in each other's arms.

I leaned away, and she held my hands as I asked, "The blood lock trapped you?"

Her chin dipped in agreement. "When I threw my shield around you," she answered, stroking my cheek, "the lock took my life force too."

"Were you … *aware* in there?"

Her chin quivered. "Yes, but I am back, and am grateful for that."

Killian stepped in close, a strength at my back that felt so natural I wondered how I ever lived without him there. As I turned toward him, he studied my face, entwining his fingers with mine. "You've come into your powers," he said.

Blood stained his neck, and no matter that we had an audience, my stomach clenched. His nostrils flared, taking in my unadulterated desire, and his mouth curved slightly at the corners. Reminded we weren't alone, and my *parents* stood next me, I cleared my throat.

"I felt four powers within the lock. My magic. The elvish magic." To my mother, I added, "I'm guessing your power."

Ari asked, "And the fourth?"

"I don't know"—I hesitated—"but I don't sense that power here now."

Zara frowned as she studied me. "You've been without your powers all this time?"

"I failed the Summer Solstice Rite," I told her.

"The high priestesses?"

"Banished me."

"Oh, Willa," she said, her voice losing its power. "I am so sorry. That must have been difficult for you."

"It wasn't all bad," I told her. The trees swayed with the breeze, the stench of death lingering in the air. "I have many happy memories growing up. Besides, I have my magic now, and that's all that matters."

"It is," Ari agreed, wrapping his arm around Zara, drawing her back in close to him, where I imagined she'd stay for a while. "I feel the elvish magic within you."

I took stock, sensing the energy simmering just below mine. "I feel it, too, but I probably need to figure out *my* power before I even dare touch the elvish."

"Wise," Zara said firmly. "There is much to investigate. I do not know what the power will do, being that your magic was trapped. We must take this day by day and see how things develop." She raised her eyebrows. "I would like to assist you with understanding your power, if you are agreeable to that."

"Yes, I'd really like that," I said to the blinding smiles of my parents. But Zara was right, we needed to take this one step at a time. A month ago, I had no parents, no magic, no lover. Even I knew I needed to process everything. As if they knew exactly where my heart lay, they opened their arms to me, and I stepped into their warm hold. "Mom," I whispered. "Dad."

"We're home," Ari said, his voice rough.

It occurred to me, then, in the safety of their embrace, that we would leave all this darkness here. I promised myself I wouldn't live in the hurt of everything that had gone so wrong, in the loneliness. I would choose happiness and stay open to love, making up for all the lost time.

When I finally stepped back, Killian slid his hand in mine and I held on tight, his magic entwining with mine, making my skin tingle. I took in the scene around me, not finding dead bodies but burnt grass where all the vampires had been incinerated. I asked Killian, "Did I do all of this?"

He inclined his head, his eyes gleaming. "You did."

My throat constricted. "Our vampires, Severin?"

"All fine," he said, brushing his thumb across the back of my hand. "I told them to leave when Zara first appeared."

"Good." I exhaled slowly, scanning the smoldering grass. "Ezra?"

Ari grunted, pressing a kiss to the top of Zara's head before answering, "He was not among the dead. When your magic made its first strike, I felt his presence leave."

I blinked. "He teleported out?"

Ari shook his head. "I don't believe so. Even with teleporting, a trace is left. Ezra vanished."

"Like Gwen and Finnick vanished," I muttered to myself. But at the dazed looks I received, I explained, "Flora was the one who took Gwen and Finnick. She brought them here."

Killian frowned.

They waited.

I drew in the deepest breath of my life, knowing I was about to break Zara's heart. I told them everything, from what happened with Flora from the moment she arrived at the Citadel and the fate of my two best friends.

By the time I finished, Zara was wiping tears away, molded into Ari's hold. "Killian," I said, "can you get word to Finnick and Gwen that I'm alive?"

"Of course," he said, stepping away, pulling his cell phone from his back pocket. With my new enhanced hearing, I could hear every word of his call to Severin, but I turned to Zara.

"I'm sorry," I whispered, reaching for her hand. "I'm sorry Flora did this."

Zara shook her head slowly, a heavy sigh falling from her lips as she squeezed my hand. "It is me who is sorry." When she released my hand, her pained stare went to Ari. "We are the reason for all this hunger for power, for all this destruction."

"But you brought peace with that power."

Her hand flew to her chest. "Mixed supernaturals are accepted?"

"Among the vampires, yes." Ari smiled.

Something very broken healed in my soul watching the love in their eyes for each other, and as odd as it was, being here with them felt familiar, like we'd always been together, when sudden screaming erupted in the night.

I was quickly tackled by two sobbing vampires and hit the dirt with an *Oof.*

"You're okay," Gwen gasped, squeezing me tight, laying on top of me.

Finnick was on my side, his arm under my head, the other arm wrapped around Gwen. "We thought you were dead, Willa. *Dead.* Don't ever do that to us again."

"I won't. I promise," I grunted against the squeezing of my lungs. "But if you don't stop squishing me, you actually might kill me."

Hesitantly, they both shifted off me but didn't take their hands away as if they were afraid I'd vanish. Hell, I clung to them for the same reason. But as they studied my face, I burst out laughing. Their eyes were bulging out of their heads.

Finnick poked at my fang. "Ah, I think you have some explaining to do."

"Yeah, I think I do."

I glanced from my best friends to my parents, to the vampire who bewitched my heart.

"Come on, let's go home, and I'll tell you everything."

CHAPTER
Seventeen

THE MOMENT ARI teleported us all back into the sitting room, Raphael appeared in the doorway, pinching at the skin on his throat, bouncing on his heels. "Willa, you're home. Please, you must come immediately."

Obviously sensing that I wanted a few glasses of whiskey and couldn't possibly handle anything further tonight, Ari snapped, "What is it, Raphael?"

Raphael rubbed his hands on his pants, tapping his foot against the hardwood floor. "I believe it's easier to show you this than explain it, King."

Reluctantly, we followed him out the back door of the house, in the opposite direction of the garden, and the moment I saw what everyone else was gawking at, I gasped. A mighty dragon with huge wings and massive claws sat in the garden, but one look at his sweet eyes and my heart melted.

"Ambrose," I called.

He came trotting over, his tongue wagging out, as if he was saying, *Look mom, I'm a big boy now.*

"He must have been the fourth power I sensed in the lock," I breathed, hardly able to believe it, brushing

Ambrose's scaly face. He purred, a loud rumbly sound, leaning into me. "His power was trapped too."

"He was there with you that night when the blood lock was sealed," Zara said. "Is this not how he normally looks?"

"No, he's always been small." I wrapped my hands around his large snout and gave him a kiss. "He never grew into his fire."

Ambrose bounced from foot to foot and then turned, lifting his head and unleashing a stream of fire, setting the treetops ablaze.

Killian chuckled, the most wonderful sound to my newly sensitized hearing.

Ari cursed, sending a blast of his power to extinguish the flames.

"Oops," I said, laughing nervously. "Buddy, that was really cool; you are miraculous, but how about we don't do that again."

Ambrose dropped to the ground with a heavy thud, shaking the earth beneath my feet, his tail wagging.

Ari huffed. "Excellent, we gifted you a fire-breathing dog."

"A *perfect* fire-breathing dog," I corrected him, throwing a glare my father's way.

Zara laughed, nudging Ari before approaching Ambrose with slow steps. She rested a hand on his head. "No matter how big or strong, dear Ambrose, we are grateful for you."

Ambrose licked her face, making my mother laugh, a sound that brought a smile to Ari's face and to mine.

"All right, yes, Ambrose is astonishing and all," Gwen said, hands on her hips, "but can we hear about *why* you suddenly have fangs?"

"Yes," I said, "but what are we going to do with Ambrose? It's not like he can come into the bedroom with me anymore."

The moment my mouth shut, magic swept across the garden with a *whoosh* and a blinding green light shot against the night sky … and Ambrose looked like my Ambrose again.

"Now, *that* may come in handy," said Killian, eyeing Ambrose like a warrior sizing up a new prized sword.

Ari studied my dragon. "He must like being little with you."

"Well, good," I said, bending to kiss Ambrose's nose again. "Because I like you being little too."

With a big, slobbery lick of my cheek, he took off toward the trees before his magic raced across the darkness and light exploded, revealing a dark shadow in the sky, another line of fire burning up the tree line.

I laughed at Ari's louder curse before I turned to Zara, torn about wanting to catch her up on my entire life and learn more about her, but also wanting to explain everything to Gwen and Finnick. She smiled and took me into a long hug. "It's been a trying night for you. Be with your friends, with Killian. We have all our days and nights ahead of us to make up for lost time."

When Ari stepped in next to my mother, he tried to shield his desire for his wife from me but failed miserably. I squeezed her back tightly. "Breakfast in the garden?" I asked.

Her smile was like sunshine on a rainy day. "I will see you, then, my darling."

We said our good nights to my parents and then slipped into the house through the back door and entered the sitting room again.

Killian went to fetch us drinks while I snuggled on the couch with Gwen and Finnick. "Before you ask, yes, we're officially a couple. It's serious," I said, "and I don't see that changing anytime soon."

Finnick grinned, slapping his hand against my thigh. "Girl, you get it! I knew it would happen."

Gwen took one of my hands in both of hers. "He makes you happy?"

"Unbelievably happy," I told her. "I've never had anything like this before, not even with Mikkel. It's ..."

Both Finnick and Gwen gave me a knowing look, but it was Finnick who offered, "Mind-blowing, out-of-this-world delicious, soul-bursting joy?"

I laughed. "Yes, all of that."

My friends squealed with laughter, and the sound was the greatest salve to my soul.

A creak in the floorboard and the warm hum of power sent my attention to the doorway as Killian entered the room. His expression indicated he'd heard every word. He handed out glasses of whiskey and then took his seat near the fireplace across from us.

I downed half of the alcohol in my glass, relishing the liquid burning down my throat, and then I began, "Tonight Ezra killed Flora." I didn't leave anything out, not of what happened tonight, not even the pain of my loss. I told them of the magic, mine and the elvish, of how it felt to become whole again. I explained my thirst for blood, but my need to still breathe. They had a hundred questions, and I answered every single one.

By the end of the conversation, my friends' eyes were wide, and their mouths hung open.

"Whoa," Finnick drawled. "All this is heavy ... but good, yes?"

The understatement of the century. "Really good, but yeah, a lot to take in."

Gwen threw her arms around me, as did Finnick. "We're just so happy you're okay," Gwen said. "That was super, super scary."

"Very scary," I agreed, holding them tight. "But we're safe, and living another day, and I'm just so glad for that."

"Me too," Finnick said with a sly smile. "It'd be a damn shame for this sexy body to go to waste."

Killian chuckled.

Taking that as their cue, Finnick and Gwen finally released me and got up. Gwen asked, "Will you guys be coming home tomorrow?"

"We will," I said, beaming. "But if you wouldn't mind opening the shop for me, that would be great." Ezra was still out there, but he'd lost his legion of vampires tonight. He'd need to regroup and recruit before taking any further action.

"I don't mind one bit." Gwen kissed both of my cheeks. "I'll be there at the shop when you get home."

"Can't wait," I said.

Gwen moved to Killian, took him in a tight hold, as did Finnick, and just like that, my best friends welcomed Killian into our little circle of love. But I knew we'd need more time together for them to truly appreciate how incredible he was.

After we said our goodbyes, and they blinked out of the sitting room, Killian opened his arms. I stepped into his strong hold, and his power washed over me.

"Tonight, I felt fear," he said, his lips brushing my neck. "It's been a long time since I felt that." When he leaned away, his intense gaze held mine. "Promise me you will never make another choice like you made tonight."

To end my life to save others. "That's an easy promise to make."

His eyes glowed bright silver. "Say the words."

I knew mine shined just as bright. "I promise to always put myself first."

"Good." Stepping back, he took my hand. "Come," he murmured, the surge of hot lust tasted spicy on the air. "Now I get you all to myself."

He led the way up the stairs to his guest room instead of mine. The moment we walked in, I sensed his magic flooding the space, soundproofing our room for the night. The heat simmering between us had intensified with my new power and vampirism.

The door clicked shut behind me as I took in the space.

His room resembled the rest of the Citadel, but all I could see was the king-size canopy bed with black drapery. His power tickled at my back as he strode past me, his magic setting a blazing fire in the fireplace, to the bedside table where he grabbed something from the drawer.

He offered me a bound-leather notebook. "Open it," he said.

I did as he asked, and the drawing I saw, alongside the date of *April 28, 1865,* nearly sent me to my knees. On wobbly legs, I went straight to the bed and climbed on top, my legs dangling off the side. "What is this?" I breathed.

Killian sat next to me, sliding his hand across my thigh, giving me a slow-building smile. "I have seen you in my dreams after I was rebirthed."

Skin tingling, I flipped through the pages of his notebook. Hundreds of pencil sketches, all in different poses, were of *me*. Every year that passed since he was turned until now, he had sketched me. "How?" I managed to say.

Leaning in close, his eye contact steady, his pupils large, he brushed his knuckles across my cheek. *"You are my gemina flamma, and I am yours."*

Like a puzzle coming together, and a heavy veil lifting, everything made sense. What Killian said had not been aloud, but his smooth voice poured into my mind.

I focused on that energy drawing us together, like a thick strand of unbreakable rope and wrapped myself tightly around it and spoke into that bond. *"Is that why, when I was first in danger, you could hear me call for help?"*

He nodded. *"Yes, I suspect so."*

A horrific thought stole into my mind. *"Have you been able to read my thoughts this whole time?"*

"It doesn't work like that. I can only hear the thoughts you project to me."

I couldn't help but laugh. *"I wondered how you sometimes seemed to pluck what I was thinking right out of my mind."*

"You'd be surprised how loud your thoughts were, having no idea we shared that connection." He chuckled softly as he leaned in, his fingers grazing my lips, increasing the rate of my heartbeat, and his knowing smile told me he heard every beat.

Facing him straight on, I asked, "If this is true, why were you so distrustful of me at first?"

"You were a witch," he said plainly. "We should not have had this bond."

"Did you think I was tricking you with magic?"

He ran his fingers through the strands of hair by my face before he tugged on them. "It would not be the first time someone has tried to trick me with magic."

The puzzle was really clicking into place. "But then you realized our bond was true when you found out I was Ari's daughter."

He was nodding while I spoke. "Yes, I suspected, and Ari sensed it, too, when he first met you, but the first time I kissed you, I knew for sure."

"How?"

"Because you felt the bond," he said, brushing the tip of his finger over the side of my neck, earning a deep shiver that had him smirking. "You wanted me the way I wanted you, but I knew you couldn't fully feel the bond, which at the time I thought was because you were both witch and vampire, and perhaps being a mixed supernatural dulled the bond, but now we know otherwise, of course."

"Because now, my vampirism is free, and I can feel the bond?"

Another nod.

I did feel the bond more than ever. Before I gained my power, I sensed Killian's magic, or what I thought was Killian's magic, but even without my full vampirism, I could still feel *him* slightly. Because now I sensed his magic pulsating beneath the connection, powerful and rich, but the link was more … *alive.* "Will we have a bonding ceremony, then?" Vampires always made their bond official, not only to their friends and family, but to the vampires' bloodlines.

His chin lowered to his chest a moment before his steady gaze met mine again. "It is my hope that you will want a bonding ceremony when I ask you, but I'm aware there is witch blood running through your veins, and I must earn your heart first." He cupped my cheek, and I leaned into his touch as he murmured, "I suppose I must do my best to make you fall madly, deeply in love with me."

"I think your plan is already working." I smiled.

"Believe me, Willa, it will only get better from here." His smile took my breath away before his mouth met mine, and passion, desire, and something raw and addictive exploded between our lips.

Desperation to feel joined clawed at me, and I knew from his jerky movements this bond rode him hard too. With vampire speed and strength, we ripped the clothes from our bodies, and my back hit the mattress, while Killian slid between my thighs. His kiss became demanding, urgent, all-encompassing, and I answered it, giving all of myself through the kiss, shielding nothing from him.

Need flooded me, pooling weight low in my body. I found his hardened length. All the stars aligned when I dragged my heat over him, shifting my hips up and down, moaning against the sweeping pleasure, momentarily blinded by the power of our bond storming over us.

Until it all became too much, and I cried out in desperation. His fingers suddenly latched on to my hips, and he thrust forward powerfully. I arched my back in a shock of pleasure.

Silver eyes locked on to mine; he slowly pulled out and thrust hard again, blazing heat deep into my core. I wrapped my legs around his waist, clinging to him as he withdrew again, slowly letting me feel every inch of him, until he slammed forward again, causing my toes to curl. His eyes flared as he claimed me, and I knew my eyes burned as bright, claiming him back.

Skin slapping against skin, his mouth dropped to mine, the strands of his hair brushing over my forehead. "I've drank from you," he growled, nipping at my lip. "Mark me."

Moaning against the pleasure, I caught his wintery pine scent, but beneath that current was that spicy smell that called to the very fiber of my being. Driven by not an urge but a demand, I brushed my nose across his neck as he thrust harder, faster, grunting, and then I trailed my tongue along the bulging vein of his neck.

When he sank deep into me, pressing against the source of my pleasure sending shockwaves over me, I sank my fangs into his neck.

"Fucking hell," he roared, wildly pounding me into oblivion as I sucked and sucked and sucked on his neck, the sweetness of his blood sliding deliciously down my throat.

Until the pleasure caused me to break from his neck with a loud moan.

With speed and force, he flipped me onto my stomach, spread my legs wide, and entered me again in a powerful stroke that sent a scream of ecstasy ripping from my throat as he sank his fangs deep into the back of *my* neck.

Then, and only then, did I truly understood the depth of our bond as my soul shattered and became reborn in his arms.

CHAPTER
Eighteen

ONE WEEK LATER, I leaned against the wrought-iron railing on the large balcony off the ballroom at the Manor, watching Ambrose flying through the starry sky, looking as big as the bright moon. My dragon had never been happier spending his nights exploring the vast land at the Manor and returning to his little size during the day to sleep on the end of Killian's and my bed. The adjustment of moving out of my apartment and into the Manor hadn't been hard at all. Killian's vampires needed him, and I needed Killian. It turned out Gwen was more than happy to move into my old apartment, considering it was rent free, and took over running the bookshop full time. One day I wanted to return to my little shop, but not with Ezra on the loose and not with my unknown powers flaring within me.

For the last week, I'd started my training with my mother, while also spending my time getting to know my mom and dad better. Life was settling again, and we'd discovered I was most definitely a defensive witch. But we also hadn't yet dug deeper into my magic. *Taking it slow,* my mother had called it, and at the moment, I was perfectly fine with that decision.

"I thought you could use something with a bit of flavor,"

said Killian, offering me a glass of champagne, crimson from the added blood.

Turning to face him straight on, I scanned him appreciatively in his tux with his hair slicked back. His gaze roamed over the waves of my hair around my face, smoky makeup and my silver dress I bought purposely to match the color of his eyes.

"Thank you." I accepted the flute with a smile, hungry for something of the metallic variety. Laughter and voices carried out through the open doors of the balcony, reminding me no matter how much I wanted to rip that tux off him, it couldn't happen now.

We had arrived back in Charleston the next night after my near death, and Killian's staff had been excitedly planning this ball ever since to introduce me, Killian's *gemina flamma*, to his guard and his vampires.

For the past two hours, I'd been introduced, doted on, and met everybody of importance in Killian's life. "You're right," I admitted after a long, *long* sip. "I absolutely did need this drink." I caught cinnamon hints of the sweet type-A blood before that sugary taste hit my tongue. I didn't believe Gwen when she told me that each blood type tasted different and smelled different to each vampire, but she wasn't wrong. The rarest type, AB, Rh negative tasted the thickest, with the richest flavor, like fine wine that lingered on the tongue with an aftertaste that lasted for hours. It was also expensive, so vampires only drank it on special occasions.

After my next sip, my hunger settling into a dull ache, Killian asked, "Are you hiding out here?"

I leaned back against the railing. "Is it that obvious?"

His lips pressed together in a slight grimace. "If this is too much—"

"It's not too much." I grabbed the front of his jacket and tugged him closer, breathing in his wintery smell. "Well, having to tell everyone to call me Willa, not princess or mistress is too much, but I can deal with that."

He wrapped his arms around me, his warm laugh caressing me. "I could send an official message informing everyone to address you as Willa," he offered.

"You could do that?" I asked hopefully.

He dropped a tender kiss to my forehead. "Yes, *we* could do that."

I considered the offer but then changed my mind. "Forget it. I don't want everyone to think I'm demanding."

One eyebrow slowly arched. "You are demanding, are you not?"

His lust hit me like a heatwave, stealing all the air from my lungs, but I didn't want to breathe; I wanted to drown in him. Leaning closer, I slid my hands over his chest. "Are you trying to tell me you don't like that I'm demanding?"

He grunted, his eyes silvering. "You will be the death of me, Willa von Stein."

I laughed, moving closer to erase the distance, pressing my soft curves against his strength. "As Finnick would say, dying from lust would be a great way to die."

"I'd rather die from satisfaction than lust." Killian smirked. "At least, then I'd know I had you."

I winked, wiggling against his growing hardness. "Can't argue with you there."

Inside the marble-floored ballroom, the live band caught my attention, the Def Leopard song, "Pour Some Sugar on Me," flowed out onto the balcony. "So, this is one of the legendary parties Gwen always told me about?" I asked Killian.

"Wait until everyone is drunk," he said, his eyes bright as he scanned his vampires enjoying themselves.

In the passing days, I'd come to learn how at ease Killian was in his home, among his vampires. How he laughed with them, and how they laughed back. How much they respected him. And how they loved living in a city he kept safe for them. It only made me adore him more.

He skimmed his finger along my jawline and chuckled. "Then you will see how legendary things become." He leaned in closer, and the wintery pine aroma sank into all my senses as he murmured, "Vampires are not as modest as witches."

I lifted my glass. "Maybe I'll need a few more of these."

Killian threw his head back and gave a booming laugh. "I suspect so."

Vampires could get drunk, but it all came down to not drinking enough blood and drinking an obscene amount of alcohol. Being half witch, two hard drinks always left me with a little buzz. Five would have me dancing on tables.

When his laughter faded, he gestured to the dance floor through the large windows. "It looks as though Gwen and Finnick are enjoying themselves."

I followed his gaze and smiled at my best friends dancing together, like they always danced together, free and wild, and loving every minute of the song. They sang every word, dancing like no one was watching.

"Your friends are …" Killian hesitated and then he met my gaze. "I see why you are so close to them. They are special."

"They are," I agreed. "I'm lucky to have them."

Killian kissed my forehead before releasing me, to lean against the railing, staring out at Ambrose chasing after bats. "On a serious note, not all balls are this modern. Some resemble times of the past."

I spotted his hard, obvious swallow. "I'm guessing there is a question in there somewhere?"

He wet his lips, nodding. "You have officially been introduced to my world, but Ari would like to introduce you as his daughter."

Observing the playful gleam in his eyes, I crossed my arms. "Which means what, exactly?"

"Since I suspect you do not know how to waltz, you will need to learn."

I snorted a laugh. "You're kidding."

"I know it seems unnecessary," he countered with raised brows, "but you will be the guest of honor that night, and it will be expected that you waltz in front of Ari's vampires and the Wardens."

"And who exactly will I be dancing with?"

A rough growl ripped from this throat as he wrapped an arm around my back, yanking me into him. He bared his fangs, but they were all for show. "Only me," he stated. "Always me."

I wiggled against him with a laugh, reveling in his strength. "Well then, I'm sure I can take some dancing lessons, so I don't make as ass of myself or out of you."

"That would be impossible, *amare*."

I smiled at his upturned face. "Are you finally going to tell me what that means?"

Leaning down, he brushed his nose against my neck, and I shivered as his magic tangled with mine. He murmured in my ear, "It means *love*."

I leaned into him, and he held me tight, like nothing would ever get through him. "If you only, and always, call me anything, call me that," I told him.

His devoted smile belonged to me, *only me*. No one ever saw the side of Killian that he showed me, and I gave him the same smile back.

Glowing eyes met mine as he lifted his head, and his hand slid across my cheek until he tangled his fingers into my hair. "If you only, and always, look at me, always look at me like *that*." He sealed his mouth across mine, his fangs piercing my lip, my blood spilling out as our tongues tangled together, and his moan echoed mine.

"Good grief," Finnick drawled. "You think a week of screwing like rabbits would calm you two down."

Killian chuckled against my mouth, leaning away. Gwen and Finnick were grinning at us like fools.

Gwen danced over and took my hand, tugging me forward. "Come dance with us."

When she pulled harder, I dug my feet in. "I will, promise, but let me finish my drink."

"Finish your drink?" Finnick asked on a burst of laughter. "Or finish drinking *him*?" He scanned Killian from head to toe. "Not that I blame you."

Killian winked at Finnick.

I laughed at both of them. "What happened to that cute bartender who couldn't stop smiling at you, Finnick?"

"Oh, I'm making him wait and earn my gorgeous ass," Finnick said and then linked his arm with Gwen's. "Come, our fangy beauty; let's make everyone jealous of us on the dance floor."

"I will, promise," I told them.

Killian smiled as Finnick twirled Gwen until they passed the threshold of the ballroom, and then Killian gathered me in his arms again. "So, what now for us, *amare*?"

I sighed up at his gorgeous face that was all mine, sinking deeply into the power all around us. "We dance, laugh, and live for a little while. And then …"

His mouth brushed mine. "And then?"

"We hunt my uncle."

Coming December 13, 2022. . .
The next novel in Stacey Kennedy's Undead Ever After
series:

Pre-order your copy today!

Thank you for reading!

CLICK HERE TO SUBSCRIBE TO MY MAILING LIST TO NEVER MISS A NEW RELEASE & YOU'LL GET A FREE READ TOO!

About the Author

Stacey Kennedy is a *USA Today* bestselling author who writes contemporary and paranormal/urban fantasy romances full of heat, heart and happily ever afters. With more than 50 titles published, her books have hit Amazon, B&N and Apple Books bestseller lists.

Stacey lives with her husband and two children in southwestern Ontario—in a city that's just as charming as any of the small towns she creates. Most days, you'll find her enjoying the outdoors with her family or venturing into the forest with her horse, Priya. Stacey's just as happy curled up indoors, where she writes surrounded by her lazy dogs. She believes that sexy books about hot cowboys or alpha heroes can fix any bad day. But wine and chocolate help too.

Acknowledgments

To my husband, my children, bestie, family and friends, it's easy to write about love when there is so much love around me. To J.T., Jessica and Kayli, I'm not sure you'll ever know how much it means to me that you listen to my plotting to make sure people will enjoy them and that my stories make sense. Your input was invaluable in this book! Big thanks to my readers for your friendship and your support; my editor, Lexi, for believing in me and making my stories shine; my agent, Jessica, for always having my back; Victoria, for polishing my work in ways I never could; Regina, for the amazing cover; the kick-ass authors in my sprint group for their endless advice and support. Thank you.

Want more urban fantasy romance?Check out the first book in
Stacey Kennedy's FROSTBITE series:
Supernaturally Kissed

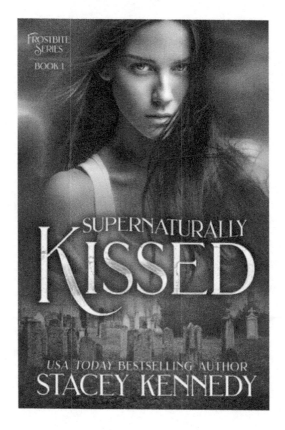

Chapter 1

An icy wisp of air swept in behind me, causing my heel to twist as I stumbled. To the other pedestrians striding along the downtown Memphis Street, the sensation would be brushed off as a cold breeze.

They were wrong. A spirit lingered here.

"Can you hear me?"

From the intrigue rolling in his voice, he hadn't expected me to acknowledge him. *Shit!* I'd already given myself away. A mistake I'd rectify.

Without hesitation, I righted my stance and strode forward with purpose, forcing myself to remain deaf to the voice. If I ignored ghosts long enough, they moved on and searched out someone else who held the same irritating ability, whom I had yet to meet.

Much to my annoyance, the ghost stayed right on my heels and his presence remained strong behind me. The cold air at my back remained a contrast to the warm morning air in front of me. Every hair on my neck stood up and goose bumps pimpled a trail along my skin. If only I could rub them away, but I didn't dare. Ignoring him would make him go away.

"You can hear me, can't you?" the ghost asked again.

Spirits were typically harmless, but annoying. *I'm dead, what's going on, why am I a ghost—yada, yada, yada.* I quickened my steps and made my way down Peabody Place in hopes he'd leave me alone.

"Wait."

He sounded desperate, which meant a big headache for me. If I hadn't worn my damn slingbacks, I would've tried to run and hide. But the three-inch Manolos and the tight, tailored gray skirt restrained my movements.

I passed Miss Polly's Soul Food Café, and the delicious aroma of bacon and eggs drifted along the air. My empty stomach complained. My only thought after I woke had been caffeine. Now I wished I'd grabbed a muffin with my latté at Starbucks. With ten minutes to get to my desk, I couldn't worry about such things.

My boss, Event Manager Dylan Cobb, would hand me my ass if I stepped into the office a minute late. Sadly, there'd never been a day I didn't cater to his every need.

I approached Beale Street and sighed in relief, relishing the warmth surrounding me. Not only from the sun above—the spirit's cold presence at my back had vanished. Pleased my dodge had worked, I took a sip of my energy in a cup and smiled. Coffee's fantastic, the ghost is gone—life is good.

Another block passed under my heels before I reached the historical red-brick building. Randall Marketing, written in black block letters, decorated the striped green-and-white awning.

I opened the door to the office and strode in, greeted by a bubbly voice. "Good morning, Tess."

"Mornin'."

"Give me a moment here." Doris shuffled paperwork around her desk, her auburn curls bouncing on her shoulders. The receptionist had always been messy, yet somehow organized. "There were a few messages on the voicemail for you." She raised her head and held out the pink slips of paper. "A lovely day today, is it not?"

"Sure is." So, I lied. The ghost hadn't kicked off my day on a high note. Not as if I'd tell her about my interaction with spirits. My ability to converse with spirits remained on a need-to-know basis, and as far as it concerned me, no one needed to know. I grabbed the messages from her hand. "Did your weekend treat you good?"

"I spent the entire weekend knee-deep in my garden." Her cocoa-colored eyes lit up. "My best year ever, I'm hoping. You'll have to come out and have a look-see."

"I'd love to." Doris treasured her gardens, so I tried to appear interested, even though my green thumb looked black.

Her smile brightened, but when the phone rang, she waved a goodbye and answered the call. "It's another beautiful day here at Randall Marketing, how may I direct your call?"

Leaving her behind, I strode down the hall toward my office and sipped my coffee. The warmth slid down my throat and provided an immediate rush to my energy levels. At the third door on the right, I entered my bleak workspace with its pale-blue walls, closed the door behind me and approached the desk. I dropped down into the black leather chair and flipped through the messages. None were urgent enough to worry about now.

I powered up my computer, but a knock at the door had me glancing up. Before I got a word out, the door swished open and I cringed, fully aware of the looming trouble.

Caley, the officer manager and my best friend since the age of four, looked like a typical Barbie. Perfect skin, long flowing blonde hair and a body men drooled over. I might have been jealous of her perfection since I couldn't pull off her looks even with a makeover—so maybe a little envious—but her appearance had always been a front. She was the devil in disguise.

She scowled, shutting the door behind her with a slam. "Do you mind explaining where you were all weekend?"

"At home." I batted my lashes. "Why? Did you try to call me?"

She pointed her finger, narrowing her eyes at me. "Don't you try that shit on me. I called you all weekend and your phone went straight to voicemail."

"Hmm…" I pretended to ponder. "The battery must have died." She had enough gall to just come over, but the little hint had been a subtle way of telling Caley to leave me alone.

"Liar." She plopped down in the seat across from my desk. "Where were you? I wanted to go out."

"Nowhere. Honestly, I vegged on the couch."

Caley snorted. "You lead such an exciting life."

My mouth parted to offer a snappy retort, but a cold wisp of air brushed across my skin, causing my lips to snap shut. Damn! I thought I'd got rid of him.

"Hello." Caley snapped her fingers in front of my face. "Leave the aliens behind and return to Mother Earth."

I blinked, trying to force my attention back to her, yet failing. The ghost knelt right beside Caley—not kneeling, of course; more like floating, since ghosts were never able to obtain physical contact with the world around them—and my focus held strong on him, unable to stop myself from ogling. He stared intently, with one crystal-blue eye, while the other was a chocolate color. His strong jaw, the muscles clenching along his cheeks, all spoke of power. But as he ran his hand through his untidy sandy-colored hair, his expression showed playfulness. His black tank top left his arms exposed and muscles upon muscles layered those arms.

"Anyways," she said, dragging my gaze back to her. "I

had to go out with Susanne because you left me high and dry."

I laughed. Caley's horny, twenty-year-old stepsister had the body that men chased after. "You did have the option to stay home, you know."

Her eyes widened. "On a Saturday night?"

"Yeah, you know, get some popcorn, watch a movie and relax."

She frowned. "If you don't stop your grandma behavior, your va-jay-jay is going to shrivel up and die."

The ghost chuckled.

His smooth laugh hit me like a cup of warm cocoa, causing my insides to melt. Nothing amused me. First off, Caley had been so wrong—maybe a little right—but I'd never admit to her accuracy aloud. Second, reacting in such a heated way to a ghost definitely didn't hit my to-do list today.

"Excuse me." I spoke not only to Caley, but also to the irritating ghost. "My va-jay-jay is just fine."

"Well, I'm glad to hear you've still got some spunk." She stood and placed her hands on her hips. "Because we've got a double date tonight."

"A what?" Dear God!

She grinned from ear to ear. "Yes, my dearest Grammy, we're going out."

"With who?"

"Two guys I met on Saturday night. You're coming with me, either willingly or unwillingly, so suck up your hesitations, babe, because saying no isn't an option."

"But it's a Monday night." Not saying a date didn't sound like fun. A month had passed since my last attempt at dating —which failed miserably—but a man Caley chose while drunk? No thanks. My sex life might have been as dead as the sexy ghost in front of me, but I'd still search for a way out. "I have to work tomorrow."

She wagged her finger in classic Caley fashion. "You're a grandma."

Most times, I respected her persistent personality. She never backed down, always dreamed big and went for the gold, but her grit hadn't been all rays of sunshine. Her determination made her annoyingly tenacious. I had to agree, or she'd never give up, and getting her out of my office sounded all too good. "Fine. I'll go with you."

"Oh, stop looking so pissy. We'll have fun. Promise. I'll come to your place at eight." She opened the door, glanced over her shoulder and winked. "Leave the granny panties at home."

———

The day came and went. My head pounded, not because my boss had been as demanding as any two-year-old, which he did often, but because the ghost hadn't shut up. The past hours, even after I returned home to get ready for tonight, he'd tried his best to gain my attention. Good thing I'm great at tuning people—ghosts—out, or I would've caved after hour two.

"I'm not leaving until you admit you can hear me," the ghost said.

With a flick of my shag-cut brown hair—that actually didn't give me any trouble tonight—to dismiss him, I strode next to Caley, heading back toward the downtown core. Dressed in my low-riding, dark wash jeans and blue plaid three-quarter-length-sleeve top, tied to leave my midriff exposed, at least I looked half decent while I suffered through the embarrassing blind date.

The ghost's tone came a little louder and more abrupt. "Dammit, woman! Will you stop ignoring me? It's annoying."

I'm annoying him. I nearly laughed at the ridiculous notion but did not intend to give myself away. I'd held strong for nine hours. Soon, he'd catch the drift and piss off.

Caley knocked my arm. "Will you stop looking so tight assed?"

I glanced away from the sidewalk and smiled at her. "My ass is tight." Okay, not eighteen-year-old tight, but only twenty-five now, I worked hard to keep things tight.

She chuckled. "You're…"

"Damn right, you do, sweet cheeks," the ghost said.

Caley stopped dead in her tracks, which caused me to stumble. "What's got you blushing?"

I righted my stance, raised my hand to my face and, to my horror, my cheeks were warm. "I'm not blushing. I-I-I'm hot."

"Unless you somehow turned into a lesbian and have fallen for your best friend, you're acting weird."

"I do love you." At her widened eyes, I laughed. "But I don't want you in the sack. Seriously, I'm just hot."

The ghost's voice deepened. "Ah, a way to grab your attention, I see."

The little purr hanging off his tone made my stomach flip-flop. Clearly, I craved some attention and needed to get some in a bad way if I reacted in such a heated way to a non-living person.

I shoved the ridiculous reaction away and focused back on Caley, falling into stride with her. "Who's the guy I'm hooking up with tonight?"

"He's just your type." She wiggled her brows. "You're going to thank me later."

"What do you mean my type?" I liked men, all types of them, and I'd never confine my options into a little box. Caley had apparently taped the box shut and shipped the package.

"He's a pro baseball player and is home visiting his family for a couple days."

"A pro, huh?" Maybe I had fooled myself into believing I didn't have a type, because hearing baseball player made my interest rise. Images of skintight white pants and a scrumptious ass filled my mind.

"Yeah, he's got the looks too." She nudged her shoulder into mine. "And the money."

"Women," the ghost muttered.

I ignored the ghost like the ghost he was, turned onto Beale Street and Coyote Ugly Saloon appeared. A line of people outside meant an hour of waiting. Not as if I thought we'd have to wait. I had Caley with me, after all.

She snatched up my hand, yanking me forward, and hurried her steps. "Brandon," she called out.

Two men turned toward her, and evidently, Caley knew my type better than I did, since either of the men would have fallen into the fantasy category.

"I'm so glad y'all came," Brandon said.

Caley gave one of her pageant smiles. "We're glad you asked us to come."

"You must be Tess."

I glanced toward hunk number two. He held the typical all-American look—brown hair, blue-eyed, charming smile, and with his dimple, I suspected he could woo his way into anyone's bed. Maybe even mine if he played his cards right tonight.

"I'm Trent."

"Nice to meet you." I ogled his trim body and handsome face and caught sight of the big white D on his navy-blue hat. "You play for Detroit?"

He nodded. "Both Brandon and I do. We were lucky enough to get a little time off to see the family."

"Figures, Detroit sucks," the ghost said.

I smiled, keeping my focus on Trent, ignoring the annoyingly sexy voice by my ear.

"Come on, let's go get a drink." Caley wrapped her arm in Brandon's and approached the bouncer. If one good thing came from her charismatic pushy attitude, she'd always been quite the social butterfly. No one, including me, ever said no to her.

"Did you grow up here in Memphis?" I asked Trent.

"Born and raised."

Seemed as if he wanted to say more, but Caley interrupted with her typical impatient yell. "Come on, y'all."

I glanced over my shoulder to find her waving her hands. "We've been summoned."

Trent chuckled.

I strode past the irritated crowd, who didn't have a Caley in their group to push their way through. Entering the bar, loud country music, accompanied by hoots and hollers, rang out around me. The stench of sweat made my nose crinkle. Caley pointed to a table across the way, and I maneuvered through the partygoers, following her.

At the table, Trent held out a stool and gestured for me to sit. He sure played his cards right to a royal flush. I slid onto the stool, and he asked, "What's your drink?"

"A cold beer sounds great."

He winked. "My kind of lady."

The boys headed to the bar. I glanced over at Caley, who bounced up and down on her seat in excitement. "I did good, right?"

I nodded, not at all ashamed to give her props for her choice. "He's not only sexy as sin, but a gentleman too. You did great."

The ghost snorted.

I'd forgotten all about him and had hoped he wouldn't follow me into the bar. Nothing would ruin my excitement now. A long time had passed since I'd met anyone worth meeting. The ghost wouldn't put a damper on my fun.

Within minutes, Trent and Brandon returned to the table with four beers in hand. I claimed a bottle, took a long sip and sighed in happiness. After the day I had, the beer comforted me. The alcohol refreshed the senses, revived the mood and removed the tension sitting heavy on my shoulders.

Trent grinned. "Looks like you needed a drink."

I licked the dribble of beer from my lips. "I've been craving a beer all day long." I set the bottle onto the table. "So, tell me, what's it like to play baseball as a pro?"

I've never regretted saying words more in my life. One question led to a twenty-minute conversation I wished I'd never instigated. Caley, the traitor, had vanished onto the dance floor with Brandon, which left me with the pompous stud.

"I've grown as a player…" Trent went on.

"This guy is a fucking joke," the ghost said.

I almost turned my head to nod, but of course refrained. I continued to listen to Trent's words without truly hearing what he had to say. I merely muttered "yeah" or "cool" when appropriate.

"If I were him, I would've skipped the conversation all together and had you back in my bed the moment I laid eyes on you."

He did not just say that! My stomach leapt up into my throat and my body warmed in places that shouldn't from a ghost. He'd only said words—not used soft touches to entice me—but the way his voice carried into my soul; the effect had been similar to sweet caresses. "The coach has been pleased…"

The ghost's tone dropped an octave. "I wouldn't have wasted the time with small talk. I would've used my mouth to learn my way around your luscious curves and used your responses to tell me about the woman you are."

I squirmed on the stool in an attempt to ignore the soft purr of his voice sending shivers down my spine. I even leaned in further toward Trent and tried to concentrate on his boring conversation.

"After I tasted your sweet skin and saw your desperation

for more, I would kiss your mouth until your lips were rosy and swollen. I'd deepen the kiss by tangling my fingers through your hair and holding you close to feel all of me."

I gulped, crossed my legs and squeezed them tight. He's a ghost! Nothing that involved him should arouse me. But the pulse between my thighs declared he held the power to make me undone.

"I'd kiss my way along your jaw while I lowered my hand to trail along your stomach. Then I would seek to discover all those little places that make you squirm."

He ran his finger from below my ear all the way to my nape. His touch forced my eyes closed. A cold shiver danced along my skin to leave goose bumps in its wake. Wild sensations stole my logical mind. My will to ignore him plummeted.

"Tess," Caley shouted.

I opened my eyes, and after taking a moment to focus, I discovered not only Caley staring at me, but Trent and Brandon too.

She frowned. "What's wrong with you?"

I shook my head and released the breath stuck in my throat, which came out in a slow wisp of air. "Nothing—I'm fine."

"I'd lower myself between those luscious legs of yours, tempting you and teasing you. I'd stare into those pretty green eyes of yours until they widened in pleasure."

"You're not fine," Caley retorted. "Your face is bright red."

"I'd wait until your hips arched toward me and begged me to take you. Then, and only then, would I give you what you desire."

I grabbed my beer, took a big swig and a couple more. All eyes stared at me with blatant confusion. Part of me wanted to move away, while the other needed to hear more.

"Ah, Tess," Caley whispered. "Seriously, are you okay?"

I paid my obvious inappropriate behavior no attention.

The fantasy the ghost built in my mind needed to have a conclusion. "Yes. Yes. I'm good."

"I would thrust against you, demanding you react to my intentions. You'd scream out and I would echo the sound with a moan of my own, as I used all my strength to satisfy you."

Caley chuckled nervously.

I gripped the edge of the table in front of me and held on tight.

"You'd come into your orgasm because I'd leave you with no other choice. But I wouldn't stop there." He ran his finger along my exposed lower back and the coldness against my hot skin made me shiver. "Without giving you the chance to recover, I'd flip you over on your knees," his tone dipped lower, "and fuck you senseless."

I shot up from my seat, which caused the stool to slam back into the person behind me, who swore in return. "I have to go."

Caley nodded. "Ah yeah, I think you do."

Without another word—or a goodbye to the living men or the dead one who had got me all hot and bothered—I bolted from the bar and ran so hard my calves burned, reminding me of the three-inch heels strapped to my feet.

The ghost didn't follow me and nothing pleased me more. I needed some space, time to return to reality or to pleasure the need out of me—either would do.

Within only a few minutes, I arrived at my condominium, which appeared more like an old textile factory, but inside were renovated modern apartments. The arousal burning inside me hadn't vanished. The wetness between my thighs was a constant reminder of the ghost's words.

I ran up the stairs while I took my keys out from my back pocket. At the thick mahogany wooden door, I raised my key pass to the scanner, grabbed the chrome door handle and swung it open.

Just three doors down, I opened the door to my condo before slamming it closed behind me. I didn't bother to lock the door and did the only thing I thought of now. I sprinted to the bedroom, stripped out of my clothes and finished the fantasy the ghost had built in my mind.

Made in the USA
Las Vegas, NV
28 January 2022